A DIFFERENT SEASON

Jennifer Heeren

Joyful Heart Publications

Joyful Heart Publications
P.O. Box 871001
Stone Mountain, Georgia 30087-0026
USA

Cover image credit: Josh Bean, Source: Unsplash

This is a work of fiction. Names, characters, places, and incidents either are the product of the author's imagination or are used fictitiously, and any resemblance to actual persons, living or dead, business establishments, events, or locales is entirely coincidental.

For everything there is a season, a time for every activity under heaven.

~ Ecclesiastes 3:1

CHAPTER 1

I ntense sadness can come early in life and Lisette Carter knew that full well. Either the walk to work was getting longer and longer or Lisette was getting slower and slower. Lisette arrived in front of the glass storefront of Bob's Diner, where she glimpsed her frizzed hair from the hot, stickiness of Baltimore in July. Her shoulders lifted as if answering her thought with, *who'll care anyway*. She pushed the door open and a crisp coolness hit her face. Lisette inhaled the air-conditioned air and a whiff of bacon.

The diner's fifties style decor boosted her spirit even in her exhaustion of being very-much-eight-months-pregnant. She headed to the kitchen to stow her purse and noticed Bart, a regular customer, park himself on a turquoise stool to wait for his first cup of coffee. Lisette smiled in his direction. Bart nodded as if to say he understood if she took a minute. Lisette's white tennis shoes squeaked on the checkerboard floor. Each day she worked was like stepping into a bright, clean, and organized world where at least one

Jennifer Heeren

aspect of her life was in control.

Lisette slid her hand over the fuchsia trim of the counter, the same shade as her uniform. Bright pink seemed to make her bulging belly more obvious. She pushed open the gray door to the kitchen and the smell of Bob's homemade buttermilk biscuits beckoned her. She breathed in the fresh-baked smell as she looked the pan over. Bob let her and Sandra have the ones that didn't turn out perfect.

Bob's dark finger pointed to one biscuit, much smaller than the others. Lisette looked up at his shiny, bald head, and then to his smile and nod which meant, *go ahead, take that one.*

"Thank you and good morning, Bob."

The biscuit may have been off in size, but it was delectable in warm, doughy goodness. After two bites, Lisette wrapped the rest in a paper towel and stowed it and her purse on the shelf. She had to get back out there and wait on her customers.

As soon as Lisette walked out of the kitchen, Sandra flounced over in her usual, exuberant tone and patted Lisette's belly. "How's my little honorary niece or nephew? I can't wait to meet you." Sandra looked at Lisette's face. "And good morning, Lisette."

"Good morning, Sandra."

Sandra Thompson, a beautiful woman, with lipstick that was always dewy fresh and the same shade of pink as her uniform. Bright shades matched her rich brown complexion. Lisette considered herself lucky if she remembered to put on lip balm. Sandra was curvy, soft and feminine but, more importantly, she was like the older sister Lisette never had. The two women connected from the first time they met.

Roger and Lisette had been like that too. Kindred spirits from the start.

Lisette hurried to the glass coffee pitchers to pour Bart a steaming cup.

As usual, the morning sped by with executives hurrying to gulp down coffee and breakfast while speaking with clients or colleagues. Tables turned over quickly in Bob's Diner.

Around mid-morning, a young, blond woman came through the front door, followed by a man carrying a baby carrier. They made their way toward the middle of the diner and sat at an empty table. She ordered a water and he a coffee while they looked over the menu.

Lisette nodded and went behind the counter to fill a glass with ice and water from the soda fountain. She picked up a turquoise mug and reached for the pitcher's brown plastic handle.

The man was doting over his child. "She's such a good baby. Even in this hectic atmosphere, she sleeps."

That's what having a baby was supposed to be like. Man, woman, and baby. Why couldn't her story be more like theirs?

Lisette's hand shook when Sandra's voice startled her.

"Are you going to pour that cup of coffee, Lisette? Someone else might need access to the pot too."

She offered Sandra first use of the pot she'd been

neglecting.

The eleven-thirty lull gave just enough time for Sandra and Lisette to prepare for lunchtime. Lisette's feet seemed to be spreading. She would love to elevate them but the bell above the door tinkled and the first lunch customer walked through. A man in a gray suit with a black shirt and black tie. His short dark hair was slicked back with gel right above his ears. He had a hint of a mustache and beard, light stubble really, that a lot of women would consider handsome.

More customers came through the doors. Lisette grabbed a menu and went over to the first. The man took hold of the laminated plastic as Lisette spouted her speech. "Welcome to Bob's Diner. May I get you something to drink while you look at our menu?"

He looked up and smiled revealing warm, chocolate brown eyes. "Yes, I'll have a cup of black coffee, please."

Lisette blushed and retreated behind the counter to get his beverage, thankful for the break from his smile and gaze. When she returned, he said, "I'd like the hamburger platter, please."

Lisette nodded and headed toward the kitchen where Sandra tapped her on the shoulder and leaned into whisper. "That guy is hot. Is he wearing a ring?"

"I didn't notice," Lisette whispered with a shake of her head.

"He's more than cute. You should flirt with him."

Lisette's cheeks grew warm as she raised her eyebrows, took a step backward, and patted her belly. "I'm in no condition for that, Sandra."

Sandra laughed too loud. "Girl, take it from me. You can always flirt."

Lisette smiled at her friend's misplaced enthusiasm. It could be the end of the world and Sandra would still flirt up a storm, but Lisette was different. She had no right to flirt. She wiped the already spotless counter in front of her. Was she trying to scrub away Sandra's silly notions or that man's face from her mind?

"Hamburger platter pick up," Bob bellowed.

Lisette took it to her customer who asked, "How far along are you?" His eyes shifted downward and back up again. "Lis-ette." She liked how he drew her name out to get it right. Some people read it as if the s was a z.

"Just a little over a month to go."

"I hope it goes by quickly. I've heard being pregnant in the summer is very uncomfortable."

"Tell me about it." Was Lisette fooling herself or did she see genuine empathy in his eyes? "It's getting difficult to be on my feet all day, too." She placed his check on the table and turned up her mouth in a half-smile. "No rush, I'm just saving myself the trip of bringing this back later."

"No problem." He gave another warm smile and a wink.

Had it been a wink or was Lisette seeing things? She figured it was the latter.

Out of the corner of her eye, she noticed him reading his iPhone while he ate his lunch. Half an hour later, he brought his check to the antique-looking turquoise metal cash register and held out a twenty-dollar bill as Lisette inputted the price of his meal. His eyes crinkled as he smiled. Lisette counted his change. $11.55.

"Thank you, Lisette." He placed the money into his wallet. He kept his wallet out as he turned to go, paused at his table, and dropped a bill onto it. After the bell on the door rang with his exit, Lisette walked over and saw a five-dollar bill lying on the table. It was over fifty percent of his bill.

Sandra appeared behind her. "Girl, he must've liked you. When a man smiles and tips like that, it can only mean one thing."

Lisette rolled her eyes. "Oh Sandra, he feels sorry for the prego working on her feet all day. It's as simple as that."

Sandra tilted her head and shrugged her rounded shoulders, "Maybe, but maybe not."

Lisette sighed. There was no chance that man could be interested in her.

CHAPTER 2

"Guess who's here again?" Sandra taunted Lisette with an elbow nudge as she passed by.

Lisette pretended to not know what she was talking about even though she had noticed that man come in again. She shook her head and dismissed her friend's over-exuberance as nonsense. Lisette walked over and handed him a menu. "Hi again."

"The food was so good I had to come back, Lisette." He spoke her name as if they were old friends. "I'm David. David Baranski." He held his right hand out as he introduced himself. Lisette noticed those warm, brown eyes again.

Another sheepish "Hi" was all that escaped her lips as she nodded and took hold of his hand. She pulled her hand away after a second and noted his attire: a dark blue suit, a light blue shirt, and a blue paisley tie had to have been the handiwork of an adoring wife. She sighed. Last year, she had done that for Roger before he went to work.

The baby's foot poked Lisette in her side, jarring her from her sweet memory. She pressed on the spot. How could such a tiny creature cause so much impact? It's like Roger told the baby to nudge Lisette because she was speaking with another man.

The man's eyes grew wide. "Did the baby just kick?"

"Yeah." Lisette replied. Why did this man care about her baby?

"It's cool to see something like that," he added. "You know, it's like witnessing a small miracle."

"Maybe...but more than anything it sort of hurts." Her lips pressed together as she continued to rub at the sore spot. Lisette wished he wouldn't speak of such intimacies with her.

His brown eyes sparkled as he smiled which seemed even more personal than his conversation. Why did he have to smile at her like that? It was rather unnerving.

She took his order. He wanted the hamburger platter again. After she put that in, she headed over to another table of two young businessmen. Grilled cheese and soup for one and a chef salad for the other. And there was still another order for a young lady in jogging apparel. She asked for a fruit plate, a bagel, and water. When Lisette had placed food in front of all her customers, she paused a few minutes to relax. Every time she got a chance, she leaned a little to take some burden off her feet. Stretching her calves also seemed to help. The man from yesterday was again eating his lunch while reading something on his iPhone. The two businessmen were bantering back and forth. And the jogging lady was nibbling on her fruit.

David finished his lunch and brought his check to Lisette instead of making her come to him. He said, "The food was good again. I'll be back."

He turned to go, paused at his table, dropped another five, and headed out the door. Lisette wondered about the job this man had that he could afford to leave such a large gratuity on every meal at every restaurant. Then Lisette's mind went where she didn't want it to. Maybe he didn't tip all servers like that. What if Sandra was right, and he was interested in her? She shook her head as she realized that was only a silly notion put there by Sandra's whims. He was a Good Samaritan-type. That's all.

After another few minutes, the two businessmen got Lisette's attention. When she walked over, one of them handed her their check with a credit card on top. She rang them up and they left. The gratuity they left was almost fifteen percent.

The young lady in the jogging clothes called her over and asked for her check too. Lisette handed it to her. She wasted no time placing her credit card on top. Lisette rung her up and she left. The gratuity she filled in was around fifteen percent.

That was the norm. Five dollars on a ten or eleven-dollar bill wasn't. What was that man trying to pull?

Lisette stopped in a downtown market on her way home from work. Some people that lived in the city drove further out to go to a large chain grocery store, but Lisette never saw the need to do that. It didn't matter anyway because she didn't have a car and carrying groceries on a local bus line wouldn't be fun.

While looking at the apples and trying to pick out a few that were unblemished, Lisette heard a very soft whimper. She looked around to see the source of the sound. Nobody had a child in their shopping cart near her. She touched her own stomach and wondered if it was possible that she heard her own baby in her womb. Then she shook her head with disbelief at that hypothesis.

Her attention returned to perusing the apples. She should have fresh fruits and vegetables in her apartment more often. Again, another whimper got her attention. The sound seemed to emanate from below the display of Bartlett pears. She moved closer and stooped toward the sound. Sure enough, there was a little girl sitting crossed legged underneath the table. She appeared to be hiding. As Lisette leaned over to get a better look at the blond headed girl with two piggy tails, she saw the little girl was wearing a dark green and white checked dress, white lace socks folded over, and green Maryjane shoes. If fear hadn't clouded her face, she would have been the perfect picture of cuteness.

"Are you okay?" Lisette spoke.

The scared little girl moved her head back and forth as her lower lip protruded.

"Are you lost?" Lisette asked.

The girl nodded and sniffed twice.

Lisette offered her hand. "If you come out, I can help you find your mommy. Is that who brought you here?"

The little girl nodded again and took hold of Lisette's hand.

"Okay, come on," Lisette smiled, "we'll go find her."

The girl emerged from her hiding place and squeezed Lisette's left hand as if she were a drowning victim grasping a life preserver. Lisette braced herself for the the little girl's grip.

"What's your name?"

"Bonnie," her frightened voice was just a squeak.

"Okay, Bonnie, we should be able to find your mommy soon." Bonnie's mom was probably worried sick over where her daughter was. She might even locate Lisette before Lisette saw her.

"When did you last see her?" she asked little Bonnie.

Bonnie moved her lips back and forth as if she was in deep thought but shook her head a few seconds later. She didn't know when she last saw her mommy. She was just lost.

"That's okay," Lisette assured her, "we'll find her. Do you want to ride in the buggy seat while we look?"

Bonnie's face lit up with a big smile which Lisette took as a yes. She lifted Bonnie who slid her legs into the holes of the buggy seat. "I'll push you through the aisles. When you see your mommy, say, 'There she is.' Can you do that?"

Bonnie nodded.

"Okay, watch carefully and let me know if you see

your mommy. Okay?"

Bonnie obeyed and looked around.

Lisette pushed the shopping cart down each aisle. When she passed another customer, she positioned it so Bonnie could see the person's face.

Bonnie recognize no one in the first few aisles but she commented on the colored boxes, cans, and bottles.

Lisette got to the middle of the store and turned down the bread aisle. She noticed a blond woman talking to a store clerk at the other end. The woman was moving her arms as she talked to him. That must be her. As she pushed the buggy closer to the agitated woman, she positioned the cart sideways so little Bonnie could see her.

She screamed out, "Mommy!"

Bingo!

A quick breath of instant relief rushed out of Lisette's mouth.

Bonnie's mom jerked her head toward her daughter's voice and sprinted toward Lisette.

Lisette felt the need to apologize. "I was just helping Bonnie find you."

Bonnie's mom squealed as she picked up little Bonnie out of the seat and hugged her tight. "That's okay. Thank you very much."

Lisette continued to smile as she watched Bonnie clinging even tighter to her mother.

The mom thanked Lisette again and carried her child away. Lisette overheard her saying, "Now Bonnie, you must stay with me at all times from now on.

You can't wander off like that."

Lisette marveled at being able to witness such a beautiful picture of a mother and child being re-united. She bit her lower lip and patted her belly as she wondered again if she was up to the challenge of raising this baby. A year ago, she would have said, *Yes, absolutely*. But back then, she had Roger.

CHAPTER 3

There was no sign of Lisette's big tipper on Thursday or Friday, and she was glad. She didn't need an extra complication in her life right now.

Sandra kept taunting her with her loud musings and very large grins. "I wonder when he'll be back in."

To which, Lisette asked, "Who?" just to get under her friend's skin.

Sandra didn't laugh though. She ignored Lisette's question and added, "I wonder where he works. And, is it close by?"

Lisette shrugged.

Then Sandra added, "I know he'll come back in. I have a feeling about these things."

Lisette got annoyed and had the urge to stick her tongue out at her. Sandra didn't know everything. When even more time went by without the man coming into the diner, it was Lisette's turn to gloat. However, she knew Sandra meant well even though her notions were foolish.

Lisette wondered if her attitude of not wanting to see that man again was canceling out Sandra's hopes he would come back in. What would be the point of him returning? He's just a customer, no matter what kind of feeling Sandra had.

Lisette reached down and rubbed the pink material covering her protruding belly button. Soon enough, she would have much bigger problems. She didn't have time to worry about such nonsense. There would be a baby for her to take care of whether that man came back in or not. Still, it would be a lot easier to put thoughts of the man out of her head if Sandra would stop with her pie in the sky thoughts.

Lisette continued to ignore Sandra's musings but that didn't make Sandra quit. She even had the gall to say, "Well, regardless of the details, I've been praying over this and God will answer."

Lisette's eyes rolled in response to that. She used to believe in the God that Sandra gushed over but she wasn't sure any more. And even if he was there, he must not be that interested in her. If he was, Roger would still be here. Why would a wonderful God take her Roger from her?

Lisette had no interest in dating anyone, but Sandra's ruminations had her looking up almost every time she heard the tinkle of the bells on the front door. She looked up half-expecting to see David. How could she be on a first name basis already? And how could Sandra perceive something about someone she barely knew? He could be an ax murderer for all she knew.

Late Friday afternoon, Sandra said, "Well, there's always next week. He was just busy during the last few days. There's still plenty of time for him to return."

"Sandra, you've got to stop with all of this nonsense. He isn't coming in because this is just a diner and there are plenty of other places to eat lunch in downtown Baltimore."

Sandra crossed her arms across her ample bosom. The golden cross resting below her neck sparkled under the fluorescent lighting. "What do you mean? Nonsense?"

She was smiling the whole time, so Lisette knew she was just pretending to not know what she was talking about, but Lisette didn't budge. Maybe she needed to get her point across to Sandra better. "I don't need to think about that man, or any other man."

"Why not, Honey? You're a woman and he's a cutie."

"It's not that simple, Sandra."

Sandra's sing-song comment made it seem so normal to entertain her thoughts even though it wasn't normal, at least it wasn't for Lisette. Her face turned as fuchsia as her uniform. "It doesn't matter what he looks like. I...I...can't."

Sandra moved her head back and forth. As she did, her silky black ponytail swung. It seemed like it was swinging to give her words emphasis. "You thought he was cute. It's showing all over your flustered, red face," Sandra teased. "And, Lisette," she paused but then added in a serious tone, "that's okay."

"No, it isn't." Lisette forced her demeanor to sober

with her indignation. "I'm pregnant with Roger's baby."

Sandra stopped wiping down a table and slipped a comforting arm around her waist. Sandra had comforted her for what seemed like thousands of times in the last seven to eight months. Lisette always felt uplifted after they talked even though that feeling didn't stay with her for long. A haze of depression always seemed to overtake Sandra's encouragements.

"Honey, Roger is dead," Sandra spoke. "I don't want to hurt you by saying that but maybe you should date again. It might be time."

The green sponge Lisette was using dropped from her hand onto the floor. "It's time? How can you say that, Sandra? It hasn't even been a year. I loved Roger. When he died, I died too. At least I felt like it. And maybe I should have. Maybe I should have been in the same car?" Lisette's eyes moistened as she bit her tongue to stifle her tears. "And...maybe I should have been because it's just too hard to go on without him."

Sandra bent down to pick up the green sponge from the black tile. Then she dropped it into her container of warm, sudsy water. She placed her arm around me again and squeezed. "Lisette, you weren't in that car for a reason. Yes, it's terrible that Roger was. It was a horrific thing to happen. There's no reason for Roger's death. But there is a reason you weren't in the car." Sandra paused and rubbed a finger up Lisette's cheek to erase one of the tear's tracks.

Then she continued, "I never meant to make you cry. I am sorry. I know it hasn't been that long, but

I also know you have grieved deeply, Lisette. There were many times over the last few months it seemed like you were dead. You were so...umm...vacant." Sandra leaned back and locked eyes with Lisette. "Lisette, honey, you've grieved enough for a five-year time span. I've been a witness to it."

"And the grieving won't stop just because you feel signs of life again. You will always feel Roger's memory within your heart." Sandra patted her chest and left her hand there. "You living again won't erase him. But Lisette...you've got to feel life again, if not for your own sake, for your baby's."

Lisette opened her mouth but only a few shallow breaths came out. Nausea overcame her. If she did what Sandra was insinuating, wouldn't Roger just disappear? She didn't want that. She wanted to be with him forever.

Sandra's eyes widened. She pulled out the nearest chair and pushed Lisette into it. "You don't look so good, Lisette. Are you okay?"

A few more breaths puffed from Lisette's mouth. The breaths were much too fast to be calming.

The skirt of Sandra's uniform twirled as she moved behind the counter. Just watching that movement was enough to bring on another wave of nausea. Sandra filled a glass with water and moved as fast as she could without spilling it. "Here drink this, honey, you're so pale."

Both of Lisette's hands wrapped around the cool glass as she brought it to her lips. One more shallow breath came out and then she could take a sip of the water. She paused and then took another sip. After another, she could speak again. "I'm okay."

Sandra's eyes looked upward, and Lisette saw her mouth a silent, "Thank you."

Lisette continued to sip on the water until she finished it and then she set the glass on the nearest white, Formica table.

Sandra blew out a puff of air. "Well, now I'm not so sure I should have said that thing about your grieving. Maybe you need more time. However, honey, I wasn't lying about being a witness to your extreme pain. I want to see you...maybe...find some comfort. That's all."

Lisette nodded. Anyone else might have ended the conversation right there but not Sandra.

"And anyway, sometimes there are extenuating circumstances and there's no prescribed grief time table for everyone. I'll be praying for God to bring you some of that comfort, Lisette. You deserve it and...you need it."

Lisette squinted her eyes, trying to comprehend.

Sandra wagged her finger toward Lisette's belly. "You may need help with this baby, Lisette Carter," she warned, and then pulled her in for another soft, comforting hug.

Lisette wiggled out of her embrace after a moment. She wanted to move away from her advice. Another silent tear fell down her cheek. Anxiousness about expecting a baby and being alone had brought Lisette as much grief as losing Roger had. Wondering if she could do it was a constant thought. Would an adoption plan be better? She hadn't mentioned that possibility to anyone yet. "It will be hard. Won't it?"

Lisette's friend's eyes glistened. "It'll be okay, and no matter what, Aunt Sandra will be there when you need her--anytime. No matter what, you're not alone."

Sandra smiled at Lisette which seemed counterintuitive to her glistening eyes and sniffing nose. Lisette had made her sad too. Her depression was so bad that even a super positive person like Sandra wasn't immune to the runoff.

After a few moments, the two women composed themselves and got back to wiping down the tables and chairs. The sooner they got the room cleaned up, the sooner they could go home. Lisette felt like going home and curling up on her sofa. Some days it was just too hard to function.

Lisette was wiping down her fifth table when Sandra looked up and spoke again. "But don't give up on someone else helping you though. I will keep on praying for more help for you."

Lisette's eyes widened at Sandra once again. Honestly, it was infuriating how Sandra was like the little engine that could.

CHAPTER 4

Lisette trudged through the door of her apartment and pulled off her white tennis shoes. The diner closed on the weekends since most of Bob's customers were business clientele. Therefore, any leftovers on Friday were available for Sandra and Lisette to take home. Lisette never ceased to be grateful for this bonus because it saved her money on her food budget.

However, that evening, Lisette didn't want food. She wanted to relax on the couch for a few minutes with her feet up. This is the weekend she'd wanted to avoid.

She plopped down on her navy couch, lifted her feet up onto the soft cushion, and clicked the channel up button on the remote. She was just looking for some white noise to soothe her tired brain. It didn't matter what she landed on. She stopped on Jeopardy.

Her mind drifted back to a year ago. This weekend was her first wedding anniversary, and it wasn't fair she was here alone with her aching feet, worried mind, and no one to help with either of those things. Roger would have massaged her feet for her, but he wasn't there. He also would have soothed her worries, but he wasn't there for that either. No one was there. Lisette was alone and lying on the couch that Roger and she picked out together, looking at the lavender walls they painted together. No, it wasn't fair at all.

She turned the volume up to let Alex Trebek's answers and questions fill her mind instead of her wayward thoughts.

"I'll take Explorers for three hundred, Alex." An older, brunette woman spoke.

"Around 1542 explorer Juan Rodriguez Cabrillo discovered this island off L.A. & it's believed he's buried there too." Alex read.

"What is Catalina?"

"Correct."

"Numbers for four hundred," the same woman says again.

"This number, one of the first 20, uses only one vowel (4 times)!"

"What is seventeen?" The woman smiled.

"That's correct," Alex affirmed.

This contestant seemed to know every answer. How did her mind work so fast?

"Now I'll take Great Literature for two hundred, Alex."

"According to C. S. Lewis, it was bordered on the east by the Eastern Ocean and on the north by the River Shribble."

The woman rang in first again. "What is Narnia?"

"Correct again. You are on a roll."

Roger was reading The Chronicles of Narnia book series on the day Lisette and he met in ninth grade. His dad read the whole Narnia series to him multiple times when Roger was a boy and Roger continued the tradition when he was old enough to read on his own. He said he always got something new out of it.

Even Alex Trebek's questions led her back to thoughts of Roger. Lisette picked up the remote again and snapped off the television. So much for distractions. She got up and walked into the bedroom hoping her thoughts of Roger would dissipate.

She picked up one of the medium-sized cardboard boxes she had shoved into the corner a month ago. The pregnancy books told her she should be nesting. But didn't nesting go along with the excitement of a new baby? Lisette wasn't all that excited about her pregnancy. At least, not like she should be. Everything Lisette read said pregnant women nest. But what if she gave up her baby to an adoption agency?

She carried the first box to the bed, set it down, and lifted the lid off. She knew she needed to pack away some of Roger's things, but it hurt every time she tried.

A year ago, life held so much promise. She picked up the silver-framed wedding picture on her nightstand. It haunted her every night since last November, but she hadn't been able to pack it away. Some people might have stuffed it into a box already. Not because they wanted to, but because they had to for their sanity. Seeing it every day was hard, and yet she still didn't want to pack that frame away.

She stared at the two young and innocent kids, ready to become man and wife and spend a lifetime together. It was just a year ago, but she didn't feel like a kid anymore. Roger wore his dashing black suit without a tie. That look was a part of Roger's style. Even on his wedding day, a tie was out of the question. She loved him and his style and thought he looked handsome with or without a tie. The top three buttons of his white shirt were undone to reveal a sexy patch of his dark chest hair.

Lisette wore a simple, A-line, sleeveless white dress with a pearl necklace her mom gave her on her thirteenth birthday. It reminded her of pictures of Jackie Kennedy—simple, but elegant—and she felt every bit as elegant on that day. Lisette's mind drifted backward.

"Are you okay, Lisette? You look a little pale." Roger *stopped me in the middle of going up the courthouse steps.*

She smiled at his impish grin and bright blue eyes. She loved him from the start of their first year in high school. "I'm okay. I'm about to marry the love of my life." Lisette took in a cleansing breath of fresh air. "I have butterflies in my belly, that's all. It's a big step."

"If you're not ready, we can wait," Roger assured her in his always-calm manner.

She shook her head, "No, I'm ready. I know I love you. And I also know those old butterflies will subside." Her nervousness seemed to fade as anticipation grew.

"They'd better. I don't want my beautiful bride to throw up on our wedding day." Roger laughed.

Lisette punched Roger's shoulder and said, "Come on, let's go." Lisette could still remember how hope for the future flooded her face at that moment.

"Wait..." Roger said as he grabbed her shoulders and pulled her toward him. Then he planted a soft sweet kiss on Lisette's lips. Her lips responded in kind.

"Roger, you're supposed to do that after the ceremony." She feigned a shocked expression.

"I couldn't wait. You're just so beautiful and you will be mine officially soon." His impish grin returned.

"Now you did it," Lisette smiled back at him. "The butterflies are gone. I am sure of this one thing...you, Roger Carter. I'm sure of you."

"I'm sure of you too, Lisette, soon to be my wife and Mrs. Carter."

The picture in Lisette's hand seemed to move with the two young adults yearning to start their married life together. She hugged the picture to her bosom. Shouldn't it have lasted forever? A year ago, it seemed like it would.

She never would have thought at twenty-three she'd have no happiness to look forward to. Roger and she should have gone on forever, but they couldn't. But Lisette had to go on because of the baby growing inside her. Lisette's small fist hit her pillow. Why wasn't Roger here, with her? How did one survive when the unthinkable became a reality? All she'd been able to do so far was just get by. Was that enough?

When the baby came, would she miss Roger even more? This wasn't how it should be. It wasn't fair. Where was God when she needed him most? She might break from this pressure. Wasn't God supposed to comfort her in a time like this?

Lisette set the silver frame back in its place on the nightstand and placed the cardboard lid back on the empty box—which she carried back over to the corner of the room. Packing her memories away could wait awhile longer. She wasn't ready to do it. But would she ever be?

CHAPTER 5

L isette was happy to return to work on Monday morning after her so-called wedding anniversary weekend. At work, she could concentrate on just doing her job. Busyness always seemed like the next best thing to numbness when trying to stop the hurt of a broken heart.

When she walked through those familiar glass doors, Lisette spied a flower arrangement full of yellow roses, white daisies, bright yellow carnations, and yellow Gerbera daisies on the counter. The arrangement was huge, beautiful and cheery.

Sandra walked out of the kitchen with Bob trailing behind her. She came over and placed a warm arm around Lisette's back and squeezed. "I remembered what this weekend was, Lisette." She pointed toward the huge flower display. "We thought this might cheer you up."

Bob cleared his throat and added, "We wanted to help you." Bob was the typical manly man that didn't handle major shows of emotion well. His shiny bald head and burly shoulders reminded Lisette of a black Mr. Clean. However, his typical gruff demeanor made his wanting to help Lisette mean even more. Gladness poured over Lisette. She was very thankful to have Sandra and Bob in her life. They cared for her.

After wiping a wayward, happy tear, Lisette smiled. That happy tear felt a lot different from the many others she had shed. She didn't have to worry about tears smudging her make-up because she didn't wear make-up anymore. What was the point in that?

"Thank you, guys, they're beautiful. I noticed them as soon as I stepped through the front doors. They're very cheery. It means a lot you thought of me like this."

Sandra and Bob smiled at Lisette's approval.

"And...if you need to talk, you know I'm always available to listen," she added.

Lisette nodded. "I know. Thank you, Sandra."

"I think Sandra can handle that part much better than me. She's much better at that emotional stuff. I'll head back to my post in the kitchen." Bob walked away like a football player heading for the safety of the locker room after the big game.

"Thank you again, Bob." Lisette called after him.

He turned his head around and winked in Lisette's direction. Then he lifted his right arm in a gesture that seemed to say, *Yeah, Yeah.*

Lisette noticed Sandra's eyes followed Bob as he walked back to the kitchen.

A little past noon, David again walked into the diner, dressed in a gray suit, white shirt, and black tie. Why did Lisette keep noticing his attire? This time, however, David wasn't alone. Another man dressed in a black suit was with him. They both sat at the same table where David had sat before. Lisette wondered why David always picked the same table. She'd be more comfortable if he sat at different tables each time.

The twinge of excitement that came over her also made her feel uncomfortable. She took a deep breath to compose herself, hoping that both feelings would disappear. These men were just customers. She handed both men the shiny menus. "Welcome to Bob's Diner. What would you two like to drink?"

Lisette concentrated on his friend, which made her feel more stable.

His friend barely looked up while he answered, "Coke."

When she turned in David's direction, she saw him smiling his usual smile. The one that made his eyes twinkle.

"Black coffee, please."

Lisette walked away, scolding herself for noticing that twinkle again. She had no right. To make matters worse, Sandra nudged and winked at her. Lisette rolled her eyes. If Sandra didn't stop with the shenanigans, Lisette might have to pinch her.

Lisette walked back to their table with an icy glass of Coke in one hand and a turquoise mug of hot, black coffee in the other. She set both in front of her customers.

"We're ready to order. I'll have the tuna sandwich and chips." David looked into Lisette's eyes, as he always seemed to do, as he spoke.

In contrast, his friend still didn't even look up. "I'll have the hot turkey sandwich with fries."

She put their orders up at the counter that displayed a view of the kitchen. The bell on the front door tinkled as a man and a woman came in and sat at another of Lisette's tables. Grateful for the distraction, she greeted them and handed them menus. She then noticed Sandra, in eavesdropping mode, as she was wiping the table next to David and his guest. Afterward, she walked toward Lisette flashing a guilty but satisfied smile.

She whispered in a sing-song cadence, "I know something you don't know."

"What?"

Sandra leaned her lips closer to Lisette's ear. "He said to his friend, 'That's her, the one I told you about.' See, he is talking about you when he's not here."

"What?" Lisette looked at her friend as if a green leprechaun just crawled out of her butt.

"I told you he's interested in you." Sandra continued, "I know these things. I have a knack."

Lisette dismissed her again as she whispered, "You're jumping to conclusions, Sandra. There's no reason to believe that's true. He probably just told his friend about the fat waitress he felt sorry for." Now Lisette was having as much fun dismissing Sandra's notions as Sandra did in teasing her.

"I should smack you, girl," Sandra joked.

Lisette noticed Bob setting the men's food on the counter as he bellowed, "Pickup."

Relieved to walk away from Sandra's insinuations, Lisette took the food to the two men.

After she set their orders down, David cleared his throat and then looked at Lisette again, "I know this sounds funny with your condition and all, but I noticed you're pretty and not wearing a ring."

Lisette's mouth fell open as a warm blush crept into her cheeks. She wondered if she should wear her wedding ring again. But she had taken it off because it hadn't felt right—not without Roger at her side. She whispered a meek, "Thank you," while wanting to run away.

"I don't know if you remember me or not but I'm David. David Baranski. I was in here twice last week, Lisette." With that, he reached out his right hand toward Lisette.

Lisette liked the fact he was humble enough to not imply that she would remember him. She offered her right hand and David took it and squeezed. To be polite, Lisette offered her full name. "I'm Lisette Carter."

"If you are married, Lisette, you can just tell me to buzz off," David made a small nervous sounding laugh.

"I...I'm not married. I mean...I was...but he died...in a car accident," Lisette stammered wondering why she told him that. Why should this man know her story?

"Oh, I'm sorry."

"I didn't even know I was pregnant when it happened," Lisette blurted again. Why was she telling him those things? Why couldn't she shut up? This man didn't want to know her whole history. He was probably wondering why he even began this conversation. Most men would run away from that kind of baggage.

However, David smiled with empathy that looked genuine to Lisette. "Lisette, I know you don't know me but if you need to talk sometime, I'm a good listener."

Why would she want to talk to a total stranger? But instead of asking that question, she said, "But...I...I'm pregnant. I can't go out on a date." Lisette then looked over at his friend who looked as uncomfortable as she felt.

"It wouldn't be a date. It would just be two people talking," David insisted but then paused a moment. He smiled an impish looking smile that reminded Lisette of Roger, which unnerved her even more. "Of course, if you want to go on a date, I'd be open to that too."

"Why would you want to go out with a pregnant lady?"

"Because that pregnant lady is very cute, seems very sweet, and has beautiful eyes. Why would I discriminate just because she happens to be pregnant?" There was that impish smile again.

Despite herself, Lisette found David's confident demeanor very appealing. She blushed yet again before she forced composure back in her voice. "You seem very nice and even charming, David, but I have to say no."

"To which part?" David prodded.

"What do you mean?" Lisette squinted.

"The date or the talking?"

"Umm...both."

David shook off her negative response. "Well, I still love the food here so if you change your mind, you'll have another chance." Then after a breath, he added, "And if you don't change your mind...well...that's okay too." He smiled the warmest smile Lisette had ever seen from a man other than Roger.

That night, Lisette dreamt of Roger in a black suit, of course with no tie, and a crisp white shirt with the top three buttons open. Lisette wore a knee-length, white, eyelet dress. Lisette stood on shiny wood plank floors that seemed to beckon her through the expansive ballroom. Roger took her hand and twirled her around the dance floor. The bottom of her dress swayed with every twist and turn. Lisette wondered if her feet were even touching the floor. Roger's hand caressed the small of her back. Many couples stood along the edge of the dance floor but no one else was dancing. It was as if it was Roger's and her turn to shine.

However, the moment halted when another man,

which Lisette could only see a silhouette of, tapped Roger on the shoulder and tilted his head toward Lisette. He spoke to Roger although Lisette couldn't hear what he said. Roger's response was to swirl her away, holding Lisette even tighter, and dancing her farther and farther away from the man. Roger danced Lisette to the other side of the ballroom until she could no longer see the silhouetted man. The only thing in Lisette's view was Roger's smiling face, and that was okay with her.

Lisette's eyes opened. Her heart was beating wildly. She closed her eyes again, willing herself to go back to sleep. To see Roger again. To dance with him. Roger's arms holding her again felt so wonderful. Everything in her wanted to go back to sleep to see more of that beautiful dream. But additional sleep eluded her. Roger was no longer by her side.

She reached for her cell phone that was charging on the nightstand. 5:02. She needed to get up by 5:30 anyway so she got out of bed. Lisette knew one thing now. She knew the dream had been confirmation she should not even consider dating anyone else. Roger wouldn't like it.

Lisette arrived at work before Sandra and filled the salt, pepper, and sugar containers on the tables. Sandra bounced through the door afterwards. A red ribbon contrasted her thick, ebony hair and pulled it back into a smooth ponytail. Large, silver-hoop earrings dangled at the sides of her golden-brown face. Her lipstick matched her red hair ribbon.

"Good morning, Lisette, isn't it a great morning?"

Sandra's voice almost chirped with joy.

Lisette forced a smile she knew didn't appear genuine. "I guess so."

Sandra's mood didn't damper with Lisette's sour note.

"It's a great morning. Mornings are a sign of new things. Every day is full of new possibilities." Sandra continued her happy-go-lucky monologue that Lisette was only half listening to. She poured sugar into the last half-empty sugar dispenser. Then she screwed on the chrome lid.

"Yeah." Lisette's forced smile disappeared as she confided in her friend, "Sandra, I had a dream about Roger."

"Oh, I'm sorry, sweetie."

In her usual manner, Sandra switched to comforting saint mode and hurried over to Lisette's side.

"It was so real. We danced. He was smiling and his bright blue eyes glistened, and even his bushy eyebrows were vivid." A teardrop slid out of the corner of Lisette's eye.

"Well, dreams can bring back nice memories, Lisette. Treasure them." Sandra patted Lisette's hand.

"But I think Roger was trying to tell me something," Lisette spoke. "I think he wanted to tell me to stay true...to him."

"Lisette," Sandra shrieked. "Your dream did not mean that. Roger would not want you to wallow in sadness. From what you've told me, he would want you to be happy. Period."

Lisette knew her dream meant something regardless of Sandra's opinion. However, she couldn't meet her friend's eyes as she dismissed her convictions. Yes, Roger would have wanted her to be happy, but they should have been happy together. There shouldn't have been a period placed at the end of Roger and her story. They should have gone on forever as a wonderful couple.

Sandra did not give up. She pulled Lisette's frame around, so she was facing her. "Look here, missy, Roger would want you to be happy, and he would want his baby to be happy too. And that baby ain't gonna be happy unless you're happy."

Lisette looked at the black and white checkerboard floor that morphed into a solid gray from the tears in her eyes. "I guess so," She muttered even though she didn't believe Sandra's words.

"Well, I know so," Sandra spoke as if she could press her conviction deep within Lisette.

Maybe it could have worked if Lisette hadn't been so dead set against it working. Roger had always told her she could be stubborn.

The conversation between Sandra and Lisette ended, but the turmoil continued to haunt Lisette's brain. She didn't want to forget Roger's face and the feeling of them dancing.

CHAPTER 6

David walked into the diner again at a little past noon. Why didn't he find somewhere else to have lunch? His dark hair was slicked back on the sides as usual. He was wearing a dark gray suit with a mauve tie. Why did he have to look so professional and handsome? His friend wasn't with him this time. He still sat at the same table, Lisette's table. Why couldn't he sit at Sandra's table for a change? Lisette needed a break from him. The situation wasn't working for Lisette at all. She walked over without smiling and handed him a menu. A dry, monotone voice came out of Lisette's mouth. She looked at the table as she spoke. "Welcome to Bob's Diner. Would you like a coffee?"

"Maybe a Coke today."

Lisette pivoted to get him his drink without looking at him. She wondered if he was still smiling at her after yesterday. Didn't he care about her opinion on this whole matter? Or did he think he could wear her down if he kept flashing that smile of his?

"Oh, and I'll save you a trip back. I'll take the BLT with fries." David called after Lisette.

"Okay." Lisette called over her shoulder as she wrote BLT with fries on her pad. After she placed his order, she headed over to the drink area to prepare his Coke. She brought it to him and set it down with a thud. She hadn't meant to set it down that hard, but the plastic glass tipped and dropped to the floor with another thud. Dark brown bubbly liquid ran onto the floor.

Lisette froze.

David jumped up and looked down at the mess.

The floor had gotten the brunt of the mishap.

When Lisette could speak again, she said, "I'm so sorry. I'll go get a cloth." Lisette moved in slow motion even though the situation called for her to be quick.

She came back with a damp cloth and a dry one and wiped the sticky mess off the table with the wet one. She tried to kneel to clean up the floor, but she could not get close enough to the ground and lifted in defeat.

David grabbed both cloths out of Lisette's hands and bent down to take care of the mess. When everything was dry again, Lisette took both cloths from him and walked them over to toss them into the bright green bucket.

When she returned to David's table, he was calm. Lisette looked again to make sure that none of the liquid got on his nice clothes. She was glad that the Coke had missed him.

"I'm so sorry," she repeated.

"Don't worry about it, Lisette, accidents happen. I'm fine." David assured her.

Lisette looked on the bright side. Maybe this fiasco would ensure that David would not return to the klutzy waitress's station anymore.

A few moments later, Ms. Wainwright came in and sat in Lisette's section. She was a regular and wore a dark skirt suit with a white silk blouse. Lisette always got a picture of a closet that was half full of multiple dark skirts and half full of white silk blouses along with a few black blazers. Ms. Wainwright kind of dressed like a man would dress if he were a woman, with no jewelry or accessories. Her brown hair was pulled back into a tight ponytail and her make-up was minimal. She probably worked in a cut-throat office and needed to portray a tough image.

"Hi, Ms. Wainwright, welcome back to Bob's Diner. Would you like your usual?" The contrast of Lisette's greeting to Ms. Wainwright and her greeting to David was unmistakable and Lisette rather hoped that David overheard and got that message loud and clear.

"Yes, please the chef salad with ranch dressing on the side." Ms. Wainwright spoke her order as if she didn't believe Lisette could remember it. She nodded when she brought it to her. She was always all business.

A few moments later, David's food was up, and Lisette took it over to him and set it down without a word.

Before she could turn to go though, David asked, "Is

something wrong? I really am okay with the spilled drink accident. I'm fine. I don't even think any got on me."

A curt, "No, nothing's wrong," came out of Lisette's mouth as she again turned to go.

David added, "I'm sorry if I made you uncomfortable yesterday."

"I said nothing is wrong." Her teeth clenched.

As if reading her mind, he asked, "Do you not want me to come in here anymore?"

"No." Lisette spoke before she thought. He was a paying customer, and she had no right to tell him not to come back. What would Bob think if she sent a customer away?

"No, you don't want me to come in here, or no, you didn't mean that?"

David's prodding her wasn't helping her feel any more comfortable. "I didn't mean that." She whimpered. "I can't stop you from coming in here."

"But you wish you could, right? I don't want to make you uncomfortable, Lisette. I never wanted that," David apologized with his brown eyes pleading.

Lisette's eyes were tired and dry. She wanted to run out of the front door of the diner and never return. Instead, she said, "That's okay. You meant nothing bad."

"But do you want me to leave, anyway?"

Those darned brown eyes looked at her again. Now she wanted to crawl under a table and hide. "No...you don't have to leave. I'll try to...umm...deal with the situation...okay?" She gulped.

Then David looked as if he might run out of the front door and never return.

Sandra came over then and stood between them like she should have been wearing a striped shirt and a whistle. She interjected in a calm, almost stern voice. "Look, this is crazy. Neither of you are mad at the other one. But you have to work something out." She sounded very authoritative like a teacher that was putting her foot down towards her unruly students.

Sandra looked straight at Lisette and then continued her lecture. "This man may come into the diner just like anyone else."

Lisette looked at the floor and whispered a meek, "I know."

Then she looked at David. "Can you come back at seven o'clock tonight?"

Lisette looked up at Sandra again with furrowed eyebrows. What was she up to?

David looked sheepish and just as confused as Lisette. "I guess so. But why?"

"Good, she gets off at seven o'clock and you two will get a bite to eat somewhere nearby and talk this...umm...problem out." Sandra's lips pressed together as she nodded as if she settled everything.

Lisette glared at Sandra. This was none of her business. "Talk what out? We don't even know each other. What's there to talk out?"

Sandra didn't blink. Her voice became monotone but remained authoritative. "He's a customer. You're a waitress. He's allowed to come into the diner any time he wants. He could come in for breakfast, lunch, and dinner every single day if he wanted to. And you must be cordial to him."

"I...am...cordial." Lisette snapped. Lisette noticed the contrast in her words and her demeanor.

Sandra lifted both of her eyebrows and stared wide-eyed at Lisette. Her orders were issued, and she didn't want to hear any backtalk.

David looked as if he wanted to leave. Lisette wished he would. He should just walk away from Sandra's rude demands and out of the diner forever. That would settle everything. However, David didn't leave. He stared at Sandra dumbfounded. Lisette didn't blame him for being confused. Nobody should have to deal with a situation like this. Sandra was stepping out of her boundaries.

"I don't want to make Lisette uncomfortable, Miss."

"I'll go. I'll go," Lisette exclaimed with exasperation. "We'll talk, okay, Sandra? Would that satisfy you?" She focused her eyes on Sandra. She couldn't look at David as she spoke.

"Yes, it will. So, it's settled now." Sandra asserted with a smug smile full of blinding white teeth.

Lisette looked over and saw a disgruntled look on Ms. Wainwright's face as if she was not enjoying this soap opera scene at all.

She asserted, "Miss, I can't wait any longer for my food."

Lisette hurried over to the counter, picked up her salad and took it to her. While doing so, she noticed David paying Sandra at the register for his meal.

He stopped at his table and dropped his customary tip before he left. Lisette wondered if he was embarrassed enough to never come back to Bob's Diner again, at seven o'clock or otherwise. She could only hope.

Then Lisette remembered that she never thanked him for cleaning up the mess she had made on the floor with the spilled Coke. He's the customer. He didn't have to do that even if she couldn't bend down to do it. But he did.

CHAPTER 7

L isette hoped that David would not return to the diner at seven o'clock. She scrubbed harder at one of the white tables, trying to get a soda ring off it while mulling over what she could say to David if he showed. She was too busy to go anywhere with him. Her clean-up duties would take a while and after that the only place she wanted to go was home. Lisette hurried to the small closet at the end of the counter to get the red-handled mop. However, Sandra reached from behind her and grabbed that mop handle out of her hands. Lisette looked down at her palms, expecting to see splinters.

"I got this, girl, now just get on out of here," Sandra insisted as she nudged Lisette toward the front of the diner. Sandra turned her around, grinned, and said, "Oh, and have a great time. You deserve it and need it."

"I don't know about that," Lisette mumbled as she reached around to untie her white apron strings.

Sandra took the apron from her. "I'll put this away until tomorrow." Then she stared at her friend as if she could see her doubting mind. "Just have fun and make a new friend. That's all. It doesn't have to be anything else if you don't want it to. And...Roger would want you to be happy. Remember that."

Lisette looked at the floor as if she was measuring one of the black twelve-inch by twelve-inch tiles. Roger would not want her going on a date with anyone else. She was certain of that. She belonged with Roger, no one else. "I really don't think you're right, Sandra."

"Really? Roger would want you to be depressed all the time?" Sandra accused.

Lisette looked up from the floor and glared at her. "That's not what I meant, Sandra."

"I don't think you know what to think, Lisette."

Maybe Sandra was right. She seemed so adamant. Maybe she had a point. Lisette sighed. She knew Sandra had her best interests at heart even if she was wrong. Maybe if Lisette humored her, she'd see things her way. "Okay, I'll go get something to eat and talk to this man and that will be the end of it. Case closed. You'll see, Sandra." At least, Sandra wouldn't be able to say Lisette refused to try.

Lisette put on her best fake smile and turned to leave while tossing a quick, "Bye, Sandra," over her shoulder. Sandra could probably read her negative, closed-off thoughts and was probably praying against them.

When the door opened outward, David was right there and caught it quickly to hold it for Lisette. He had taken off his jacket and tie and looked more casual than this afternoon.

"Good evening, Lisette." The nervousness from this afternoon was gone. He looked handsome and gentlemanly. The top two buttons of his dress shirt were unbuttoned but, unlike Roger, David's chest hair wasn't showing.

"Good evening." Lisette was suddenly nervous about the fact she was still in her pink waitress uniform. The apron was gone, but it was still obviously a uniform. She smoothed down the fabric at her sides. "I'm sorry but this...umm...outing wasn't planned so I don't have a real outfit to wear."

David looked at Lisette directly. "Well, Burke's has wonderful food and it doesn't require fancy attire. And, you look great anyway." He gave her that wink she was almost used to seeing.

Lisette tried to give a slight smile even though she was nauseous.

David pointed to her right to let her know which way they'd be heading. "Burke's is also just a block away. I thought we could get something to eat there so you wouldn't have to walk far. Shall we go?" He bent his left arm at his side as if he was offering Lisette his elbow to hold on to.

She nodded yes but didn't take hold of his elbow.

His arm straightened with the rejection. They walked toward the restaurant silently.

Burke's had the best German food around. As they walked through the corner door, a delectable smell filled Lisette's nose. She couldn't place what it was but her hollow stomach seemed to yearn for it.

She used to like coming here with Roger. His smiling face came into her mind. She gulped. No...Roger wouldn't like this scenario one bit.

He had always liked German food and said Burke's was the best. They had ordered their jumbo onion rings to share as an appetizer. Why couldn't it be Roger with her now? They would have a delightful dinner as they talked about their baby's future. Lisette sighed.

David broke into her daydream. "Do you not like German food? We could go somewhere else."

"I...uh...I...I do like German food. Umm...Burke's is fine...I guess."

"Would you rather go somewhere else?"

"No, no, we can eat here. It smells delicious." She looked down at her feet.

A waitress seated them in a booth. The bench seats were dark wood, maybe mahogany or maple. The table was the same color but there was a plastic laminate sheet sealed to the top. A small, dim lamp with a brown lampshade was affixed to the wall over the table.

The waitress looked at Lisette's uniform and smiled as if they were kindred spirits. Embarrassed, Lisette ignored her look and picked up her menu. The dim lighting caused Lisette to squint to read the entrees.

"Can I take your drink orders while you peruse our menu?" the waitress chimed.

Lisette looked up and said, "Just water for me please."

"A Coke," David replied.

The waitress nodded and walked away.

Lisette glanced upward after a couple minutes to peek at David while he was looking down at his menu but instead, she caught him looking right at her. Her eyes darted back to the words pan-seared chicken.

"I don't mean to make you nervous, Lisette," David apologized. "I was just noticing how pretty you are."

"Why do you keep saying that? It makes me uncomfortable."

"I want to give you a compliment." David's confident grin turned sheepish. Although he had a confident manner about him, he also seemed to have an insecure side.

"But you shouldn't be doing that."

"Why?"

"I...I'm married."

David shook his head in confusion. "What? You are?"

Lisette's eyes moistened. "Well, yes...he died but...I'm still married...at least I would be if he was still here."

"Sometimes I don't think before stepping out." David paused a moment. "I should have realized you were still grieving. It hasn't even been a year." David breathed in a long deep breath before continuing. "But my offer still stands. We can just be friends and talk. This doesn't even have to be considered a date. You never even have to see me again if you don't want to. I'll even find somewhere else to eat lunch if you prefer."

Lisette sniffed to hold back some moisture that was forming in her nose. She didn't want to make him feel bad. "You don't have to find another lunch place. I can deal with...umm...things. And...I could probably use another friend. You seem nice." Her mouth widened into a natural smile.

"Okay, then we're just friends. That's settled. Now let's decide what we want to eat," David spoke reassuringly, "And I'm famished. Are you?"

Relief flooded through Lisette's whole body. Just friends sounded like a wonderful arrangement. She enthusiastically nodded that she was hungry.

"You seem like a nice person, David, and you have a very warm and friendly smile and demeanor." Lisette tried to relax and not worry too much about David's intentions now that they were just going to be friends. A fifty-pound weight fell from her shoulders. Suddenly, she remembered to add, "And...thank you for cleaning up my spilled soda today. You really didn't have to do that."

David smiled and even blushed a little. "It was no problem at all. But, thank you for acknowledging it. You're an easy person to be nice around, Lisette."

The same waitress that seated them walked back over. Even in the dim lighting, Lisette noticed her brown hair was graying on the sides. There was also a dark mole in between her mouth and her left cheek.

"Would you like to order an appetizer before your

meal? Our jumbo onion rings are a favorite item for two people to share."

Lisette thought of Roger and couldn't fathom sharing that same appetizer with David. It didn't feel right. "No, thank you."

Lisette saw disappointment in David's eyes even though he nodded in agreement and said, "No, but I think I'm ready to order my meal. Are you, Lisette?"

Lisette looked down at the menu again and spoke absentmindedly, "Umm...yes, I think I could order."

The waitress smiled and waited.

"I'll have this." Lisette pointed at an entrée. "The chicken breast with mushroom sauce."

"One of my favorites," the waitress remarked. "Would you like soup or salad with that?"

"Salad, please."

The waitress nodded again and then looked over at David.

"And, I'll have the grilled Black Angus steak with a salad."

The waitress again nodded. Her medium length hair swung back and forth as she took our menus away in a graceful swoop.

"You know what I do for a living, David. How about you? What do you do?" Lisette wanted to keep the conversation about David as much she could. She'd said enough already. David didn't need to know any more details about her life.

"I'm a lawyer. Well, I'm just beginning. I graduated from law school last year."

"Oh...Roger and I graduated college last year," Lisette blurted out.

"What did you two major in?" David asked.

"Roger majored in accountancy. He loved working with numbers." A smile grew on Lisette's face in just mentioning Roger.

"And you?" David prodded.

"Oh, I majored in English, that's all. David was the smart one." Memories twirled in Lisette's head. "He would have really done something." She looked down, her smile disappearing. Then she repeated with a gulp, "Would have."

David looked uncomfortable and cleared his throat. "Lisette, English is a good major too. What did you want to do?"

"I...I hadn't decided. Roger always said I could write well but I don't know. I never knew what I wanted to do with my life. I picked English because I thought I could do it." Lisette shrugged her shoulders. "Well...Roger thought I could do it."

David's tone raised an octave. "Well then, if Roger had a great head on his shoulders and he thought you could write, then you must write well."

She tilted her head and shrugged again slower this time even though David's compliment didn't ring true.

The waitress returned to the table and David paused long enough for her to set down the salads.

She picked up a tall mahogany brown pepper grinder from her tray. "Fresh pepper?"

Lisette nodded.

David said, "Yes, please."

She turned the crank as fine white pepper fell onto first Lisette's salad and then David's. Lisette knew it was white pepper because her nose twitched twice.

Before the waitress turned to go, she said, "I have to remark on what a cute couple you two are. Is this your first child?"

Lisette strangled on the bite of lettuce she'd just put into her mouth and coughed loudly.

David said to the waitress, "It's not like that, ma'am, we're just friends."

Lisette's coughs slowed down as she noticed the waitress's confused look. The waitress's reply was a simple, "Oh," before she turned to go.

Mistakes like that were why Lisette didn't want to have dinner with another man. People would assume they were a couple. Lisette didn't want to deal with those assumptions.

David didn't let the pause stop his persistence. He changed the subject. "Every time I see you from now on, I'll ask you if you wrote anything. It doesn't have to be anything big. Even a journal entry or two might help you remember your schooling."

"I got A's in Journalism. We got married right after college and then we moved downtown. It took months to settle in. And then...and then...," Lisette stopped mid-sentence.

David let out a long sigh. His eyes seemed to search her face for answers.

After a long pause of Lisette dabbing at her eyes with her napkin, David didn't press her for more information about what happened to Roger. He continued the previous topic. "Writing might help you in another aspect too. To get things out of you in a place that no one else will see."

"I don't know. I can't think clearly."

"That doesn't matter. Whatever you write is just for you." David paused. "It would be therapeutic. Everybody needs to get things out of them sometimes and after what you went through, well, you know."

Lisette sniffed. "I guess, you're right. I am kind of a mess."

"I didn't say that."

"Well, I am." Her counterfeit grin didn't even fool herself.

"Everything you're going through is perfectly normal, Lisette."

David's smile made Lisette feel understood. "Maybe, but other people can shake things off quicker than I can."

"Big things like that take a lot of time for most people to get back to normal. Everybody has trouble dealing with tragedies. They're difficult for everyone."

Lisette wondered if she could believe the empathy she saw in David's eyes. "I guess so." She took a deep breath, eager to change the subject. "So, you're a lawyer?"

"Yes, I'm a lawyer and I think I've decided to specialize in adoption law. There are so many rules and regulations out there that it makes it tough for both the people wanting to adopt and the person making an adoption plan for their baby. I would like to make the process easier for all involved if I can."

"That's great, David. You really are a nice guy." She laughed. "Are you like Superman under that suit? You know, fighting for truth, justice, and the American way?"

David snickered and feigned a look of surprise. "How'd you know? Did you see me at the phone booth down the street?"

Lisette laughed again and shook her head. "How could I have seen you in a phone booth? There aren't many anymore. Superman doesn't have anywhere to change." Lisette laughed again at her own joke. David laughed with her. Laughter felt good. Roger and Lisette used to laugh at their private jokes all the time.

"Seriously though, I'm not perfect, I care about this issue. You see, I was adopted. Therefore, I know how positive an adoption plan can be. I had a great upbringing. The parents that raised me were my real parents in every way but biological." David's brown eyes twinkled as he spoke.

"Did you ever want to know who your real parents were?"

"That's not important. My parents were the ones who chose me and loved me. I can't complain."

"I don't think it is that easy for everyone who is adopted, David."

"Most adoptions turn great kids into pretty good adults with no problems."

Lisette pondered what David was saying. Then she patted her belly. "That's really encouraging to hear.

You know, I've been thinking of possibly giving this one up for adoption."

David's mouth fell open. "Do you really want to do that, Lisette?"

"Sometimes no but sometimes yes. And, I thought you told me that adoption is a great thing?"

"It is great when it's right but, I think you'd be a great mom, Lisette. Don't do anything you might regret."

"But I might want to give my baby a better life." Lisette wondered why David was so adamant. Why did he care if she gave up her baby?

"Well, don't make any rash decisions. Think about it thoroughly," David insisted.

"But for single parents like me, it could be right, to give up a baby for adoption, right?" She questioned.

David looked away from her as if he didn't want to say the wrong thing. "Well, maybe."

"My baby could bring happiness to some couple and it would be relieved to have two parents instead of just one."

"Just don't decide that too quickly. Make sure it's right." David spoke with confidence.

"I'm not deciding right now, David," Lisette defended. It wasn't any of his business.

David looked relieved. "Good, Don't."

In a much-needed diversion, the waitress carried their entrees to the table. She still seemed a little embarrassed from her earlier faux pas. She set the chicken dish down in front of Lisette. When she did, Lisette caught a whiff of the bay leaf garnish. David's steak sizzled as his food was placed before him.

David and Lisette were quiet for the next few minutes except for a few impulsive remarks over the deliciousness of the food. As soon as they were finished eating, the evening would be over, and Lisette was thankful. David was probably used to dating girls who were more fun and cheerful, not to mention skinnier.

David attempted more conversation though. Lisette had hoped that he would have just asked for the check and then they could've been on their separate ways and away from this awkward date, meeting, or whatever it was.

"I can tell you really loved Roger, Lisette. One of two emotions show on your face when he is a topic of conversation. Sometimes you are sad in a way that makes people empathize with your loss. And at other times, you're in a blissful almost euphoric state that makes people want to share your good memories."

Lisette longed to speak about her sweet Roger. "Thank you. The way you say that makes me feel you may actually understand me."

"I think I do. You are a special lady, Lisette Carter."

Lisette's cheeks grew warm again. Why was she always blushing around this man?

David seemed happy with her reaction. "You and Roger must have been a special couple."

"We met in our freshman year of high school. His family had just moved to town, so he was the new boy in school. Many of my classmates wanted to date him. For the life of me, I'll never know why he asked me out."

What was wrong with her? One minute she wanted to end this dreadful date and the next minute she was extrapolating on her relationship with Roger.

"Oh, I can see why," David ventured, his tone oozing admiration which caused Lisette's cheeks to brighten even more.

"Stop that." She reached up her hand and smacked at the air over the table.

"What?" he said with that darn playful smile of his.

"Making me feel embarrassed." She quipped.

"Okay, okay, continue your story about you and Roger. I'll behave."

Lisette breathed in a cleansing breath and proceeded. "We met in Algebra class. He was brilliant in that class. Me, not so much." Memories flooded in and Lisette yearned to return to those days. Roger and her running around without a care in the world. "But he helped me. We went to the library after school, so he could help me with my Algebra. After the library, we'd walk across the street to get a slice of pizza at this little market. Then we went to the library after school just to do our homework together in all our subjects. We went out throughout high school. We were the typical high school sweethearts."

"And you were voted best couple, right?"

"No, the captain of the football team and his girlfriend got that honor even though Roger and I were actually together longer than they were. But they got more attention."

"You were robbed." David teased me. "I'll call up the

alumni committee from your class and complain."
Lisette laughed.

"Well, anyway..." She wanted to speak more about Roger now. She liked to talk about Roger.

David stuck up one hand. "Wait, just a minute before you continue. Do you want to split a piece of Burke's famous chocolate cake with me? It's so rich. I can't eat the whole thing."

"Sure, how can I say no to chocolate? I'm a woman and I'm pregnant so I have double the chocolate craving hormones in me." She smirked.

David waved for the waitress and ordered the decadent dessert. Then he paused and said, "Okay, now go ahead. Continue."

"Well, we went out all of high school and then we both commuted to Towson University, so we also were together all four years of college."

"That is a long time. A lot of high school couples don't stay together afterward."

"Actually, we ended up living together in our sophomore year of college."

"Hmm...now we're getting to the juicy part." David snickered.

"It wasn't like that," Lisette insisted, "After my high school graduation, my mom got this wild hair to move to California of all places. She wanted to start her life all over again and since I was over eighteen, she felt she had every right to do it. Actually, to be fair, she asked me to go with her, but I didn't want to go to California. I wanted to stay in Maryland and continue to date Roger."

"How about your dad?"

Lisette gulped. "When I was thirteen, Dad and Mom announced their divorce and he moved to Texas. I never heard from him again."

"That's terrible," David said.

Lisette nodded.

David changed the subject, "Is that when you and Roger got married?"

"No, I moved in with Roger and his parents. They had a small studio apartment built into their basement and I stayed there." Then she added, "Roger was upstairs in his room."

"Didn't he sneak down?" David gave another playful look.

"At times, but not like you're thinking. Roger's parents were strict. We were actually very chaste." Lisette looked away for a moment but then smiled. "Actually, Roger's parents weren't the only thing that kept us innocent. It was me too. When I was a preteen, I was taught it was better to wait. I know that sounds silly but..."

"No, that is definitely not silly." David interrupted. "I think it's refreshing. Especially, in this day when girls get pregnant at fourteen years old."

"Well, right or wrong, I waited. Four years of high school, four years of college, then we got married last year in July. The waiting made our marriage feel even more special." Lisette tapped her belly. "And if this is a girl, I hope she waits for marriage too."

The server brought out the piece of rich, dark chocolate cake with two forks and set it in the middle of the table. "Everyone loves that cake," she remarked before she turned to go.

Lisette's eyes grew larger as the aroma of the dark chocolate invaded both nostrils. "But I'm not waiting for that." Then she picked up a fork and dug in to get a large bite.

David laughed. "Me neither." He dug into the tower of chocolate too.

When there was nothing left but crumbs, they both leaned back on their prospective sides of the booth.

Lisette spoke up first. "You're right, I couldn't have eaten a whole piece of that delicious monstrosity by myself, but I might have liked to try." She giggled to punctuate her gluttonous thought.

"Mmm hmm," David concurred with a satisfied smile.

A few moments later, the waitress set their check onto the table. Lisette reached for her purse.

"No...no...I got this, Lisette." David blurted.

"But David, we decided that we're just going to be friends." Lisette pleaded as she continued to reach inside her purse for her wallet.

David smiled. "Well, I can buy my friend dinner, can't I?"

"But..."

"No buts."

Lisette didn't think she could win the argument, so she gave up and closed her purse.

David seemed satisfied with her withdrawal and placed his credit card inside the black leather folder.

Defeated, Lisette said, "Well, it's probably for the

best. I've been trying to save every little bit of money I can for future baby needs."

"Well then, this will help, won't it?"

CHAPTER 8

The next day, David walked into the diner at lunchtime, carrying a pink package tied up with a shiny, white ribbon. He set the package down on his customary table and took a seat himself. Sandra's eyes widened as she noticed the package. She nudged Lisette's arm and whispered, "Well, well, well, last night must have gone pretty well."

"I told you, Sandra, we're just going to be friends." An emphatic whisper came out of Lisette's mouth.

"Umm hmm," Sandra spoke as she shook her head to erase Lisette's declaration. "Does he know that?"

"He does. He's the one who said it."

"Did he mean it?"

Why wouldn't Sandra drop those crazy notions? "Yes, of course he meant it." Lisette pushed Sandra's arm away. "Now, shh...I've got work to do."

She greeted David with a friendly, "Hello." Lisette's eyes were drawn to the exquisitely wrapped package as she wondered if Sandra might have a point.

David greeted her in return and ordered a tuna

sandwich and coffee without wasting a minute. He didn't even mention the pretty, pink package.

Lisette gave Sandra a knowing nod as she brushed passed her. "See, the package isn't even for me. He didn't even mention it."

Sandra's eyes squinted. "That's weird."

"There's nothing weird about it. I told you. We're just friends. That pretty pink and white package is probably for some other girl."

After receiving a call on his cell phone, David ate his tuna sandwich quickly and paid his bill almost as fast. Lisette was busy taking another customer's order when out of the corner of her eye she spotted David giving his bill to Sandra who rang him up. Then just two minutes later, Lisette looked up when she heard the bell on the front door. David was gone.

Lisette supposed that now that he knew where they stood in their relationship, or lack thereof, he would move on to some other girl who could offer him more. She would probably appreciate that neatly wrapped pink package.

Lisette's insides were numb as she slowly walked over to clear off his table. Her eyes widened as she noticed the pink package still sitting there on top of his usual five-dollar tip. The tag on the package read, "To: Lisette Carter, from your friend, David."

The package had been for her. She placed the five-dollar bill into her apron pocket and carried the package behind the counter to stow it for safekeeping. Even though the package was for her, David had written *your friend* on it, so he did understand her wishes.

Lisette went back to finish clearing off his table then she waited on another customer. Then another. And another. The afternoon flew by. When the customers lessened, an exasperated Sandra spoke up. "Are you going to open that package or what?"

"Yes," Lisette remarked.

"When?"

As if she didn't hear her friend, Lisette kept on wiping tables and taking orders, because she knew she was getting under Sandra's skin and it was fun. Sandra was always kidding around with her, so it was nice to turn the tables on her.

As Lisette was getting ready to leave work for the night, she picked up the package and headed toward the door when she glimpsed Sandra's pouting bottom lip.

"You're not going to open that here?" she asked.

"I was just going to take it home. It's not a big deal, Sandra. Whatever it is, it's just a friendly gesture."

Sandra's sad expression turned into a pitiful one. Lisette knew she was feigning it, but it still made her feel a twinge of guilt for holding out on her. "Okay, okay." Lisette huffed as she set her purse and the package down on the nearest table. "But it's really not a big deal at all."

Sandra stepped closer, her face beaming. "Well, we'll see about that after you see what's inside the package."

She sat down and tugged at the white ribbon. When that was loose, she ripped into the pink paper to unveil a different shade of pink in the form of a fuchsia book. When she opened the front cover, she discovered it was a lined blank book. On the heavy piece of paper before the lined paper began, David had printed, *Just something to write out your feelings and ideas--just for you. But if you ever need to talk, call me.* Below that he had written his phone number, and below that was his name.

Sandra's enthusiasm deflated. "It's pretty, but why did he give it to you?"

Lisette looked first at the book in her hands and next at Sandra. Then she shrugged even though she knew why David had given her this gift. She also knew she would never call that number even if they were just friends.

Lisette returned to her one-bedroom apartment that night and brought the fuchsia book into her bedroom. The thought of writing something in it appealed to her. She remembered how fun it was to jot things down in diaries as a kid and journals as a teen. She was once a pensive, happy girl. That was when she still had good things to write about.

She got up and went out to the living room to her desk where she found a red pen in the top drawer. She tested it out on a sticky note pad. The pen wrote smoothly, so she headed back to the bedroom with it where she sat cross-legged on the bed, reached for the journal book, and leaned it against the top of her great big belly. Lisette opened to the first page and wrote the date. Then she sat there for five minutes staring at the almost empty first page. Nothing came to her mind to write. She had nothing important to say. She soon gave up and closed the book. Then she placed both it and the pen in the drawer of her oak nightstand. Just because she used to enjoy writing in school didn't mean she would enjoy it now. Things were different. She wasn't that happy, young girl anymore. No, she was much different.

She saw Roger's face in her mind. His blue eyes twinkled, and his smile was bright. She reached her hand up to touch his face but only felt air. Now, she was even seeing things. Was this what it felt like to lose your mind?

She walked to the dresser to get her turquoise nightgown. As she slipped it over her head, Roger's face was still in her mind. Lisette got into bed with his face accompanying her the whole way.

Lisette whispered to the darkened room, "Roger, I need you. Why aren't you here? Why aren't you with me? I know what happened. But why? Why did it happen? Why did it happen to you? To us?"

The response to Lisette's pleas was a bone-chilling silence. She shut her eyes as she yearned for the deep rest of sleep.

The three words that David had written in that book came to her mind. *Just for you.* She opened her eyes again. However, she still didn't feel like writing anything, not even just for her. Maybe, she was afraid to. Afraid that she'd get lost in all the sadness and wouldn't be able to function anymore. If she wrote about it, the depression might envelope her. She couldn't let that happen. She had to keep functioning.

It was easier to do that without too much emotion getting in her way. Going through the motions was a much safer way to go through life.

Her exhausted body and mind fell into a deep slumber.

David walked into the diner the next day and apologized. "Sorry I was in and out so quickly yesterday, Lisette. I only had a little time allotted for my lunch because of a meeting I had to get back for."

"That's okay, I was busy and didn't even notice," Lisette spoke with as much nonchalance as she could muster. "Do you want a coffee today?" David was probably wondering about her reaction to his present but if she stayed silent, maybe he'd stay away from the subject. At least Lisette hoped he would. He shouldn't be buying her presents, anyway.

David's brown eyes squinted. "Yes, please. Umm... did you get the package?"

Lisette gulped and attempted to continue her casual demeanor. "Uh...thank you." Then she pivoted to get his coffee.

When she returned with the steaming mug, David persisted. "Did you like it?"

"It was very pretty."

"Good, but more importantly, did you write in it?"

Lisette could almost see the hope in David's deep brown eyes and didn't want to disappoint him. "I...I... didn't have time last night." She looked away from those eyes of his that seemed to penetrate through her. She focused on the floor.

David picked up her hand to give it a quick but gentle pat, then released it which Lisette was thankful for because she would have had to yank it away from him. His touch was a little too comforting.

Her reaction alarmed David. "It's okay, Lisette, there's plenty of time for writing in it."

She nodded. Doesn't he realize how uncomfortable he was making her? She walked toward the kitchen. As she did, those oh-too-familiar tears threatened to flow. Would she ever be able to interact with people without thinking of Roger and crying?

When Bob yelled that David's sandwich was ready, Lisette leaned toward Sandra and whispered. "Will you take this over to him for me?" Lisette didn't think she could handle this friendship. It was too hard.

Sandra reached up, squeezed her shoulder, and nodded as she picked up the plate with the sandwich. Lisette was glad that her friend seemed to understand.

"Lisette isn't available now. She asked if I could cover for her." Sandra spoke loud enough for Lisette to overhear even from her stance right inside the kitchen.

"Is she okay?" David questioned.

After that, Sandra and David's voices were too low for Lisette to hear. Lisette strained her ears, but she couldn't make out anything. She made a mental note to ask Sandra when David left. She had just asked Sandra to take him his food, not delve into his psyche.

David left the diner soon after their talk with a

half-eaten sandwich left on his plate. Sandra carried the plate into the kitchen then she handed Lisette a five-dollar bill.

Lisette attempted to give the bill back. "I...I didn't do anything. You keep it, Sandra."

Sandra shook her head and crossed her arms in front of her hourglass figure. Lisette knew she would not accept the five back, so she gave up trying. She then swallowed hard before asking, "What did you say to him, Sandra?"

"I told him you were a little confused right now and that he should bear with you."

"That's all? What did he say?"

"He said to tell you he didn't mean to push you. He only wanted to help." Sandra's tone challenged Lisette. She already knew that David wanted to help her, but she didn't think she could handle the situation.

Lisette grew quiet for the rest of the afternoon. Sandra didn't seem to know how to respond to her and that wasn't typical of her either. Sandra was never at a loss for words and never walked on eggshells around Lisette's sadness. Lisette took it as a good thing though because she didn't want to hear Sandra's input or advice.

Why did David have to walk into this stupid diner in the first place? And, why did he keep coming back? There were plenty of other places to eat lunch in Baltimore city.

And now he knew they could only be friends so what was in it for him to keep coming back? Lisette guessed that he felt obliged to help her or something, but she didn't need his charity. Her life was much easier before he showed up.

CHAPTER 9

Everything got back to normal. David did not return the next day or the next or even the one after that. No other customers asked out the tired, pregnant lady. Yes, everything was back to normal. Lisette was glad.

Now, all she had to worry about was how to ease the pains in her feet and back. It was getting harder for her to do that and perform her waitressing duties as the days drew closer to her due date. But it was too soon to stop working. She had to keep working as close to her due date as possible so she could pay her bills.

One day, Sandra sat Lisette down for a talk. "Lisette, you can take time off in the last few weeks of your pregnancy if you need to. Bob already gave his blessing for any rest you need."

"I don't see how I can, Sandra, I will already be taking maternity leave for two months after I give birth. I only get that much paid leave."

"You know Bob, Lisette, he'd let you take a year off

if he could afford it."

Lisette glimpsed the shine on Bob's slick, bald head as he worked in the kitchen. "Bob has been very nice but I don't want to take advantage." She paused and looked down at her swollen ankles. Then she added with hope in her voice, "Do you think he could afford it?"

"He would get by, business has been good, and it shows no signs of slowing down."

Lisette's face lost its glimmer of hope. "But...then you'll need the help during the day. I don't want to be a burden on you either."

Sandra sighed and stood up with straight posture and her shoulders pulled back. "I'm a strong woman. Don't you worry about good ol' Sandra. I'm like a hot cup of chai tea. The hotter the water I'm in, the more my fragrant aroma comes out. I'll thrive, girlfriend."

Lisette couldn't help smiling at her best friend's enthusiasm. "Well, maybe the diner and you could handle my absence, but can I afford to be out that long?" Lisette paused and considered how good a little more rest would feel. She continued more for her own benefit than anyone else's. "Maybe I could leave at three or four each day? The last part of the day isn't as busy, so I wouldn't feel like a complete burden on you or Bob. And it would give me more of a chance to rest each evening and I'd still be making money to pay my bills?" Lisette breathed a sigh of relief at the possibility of resting more. "I'll go home tonight and figure out if it's possible."

Sandra looked at Lisette, smiled, and nodded. Then

she added, "I'll be praying you can do it."

"Thanks, Sandra."

When Lisette got home, she went online to her bank account to look at the bills she paid in the past month or two. She had been living off less than she brought in each month. In addition, she still had the money from Roger's life insurance policy with his workplace. She had placed that money in a second savings account and had vowed not to touch it. It was for emergencies only, and dire ones at that. Lisette's frugality, as well as her lack of desire to do much outside of work, had enabled her to pocket a good little bit in her regular savings account. It allowed her some breathing room to cut back on hours for the next few weeks. After the baby came, she'd need even more money, but she didn't want to think about that right now. No, that was for another day.

Bob agreed to the proposed new work hours and thought it was a great idea. He even tried to get Lisette to take more time, but Lisette would not budge. Leaving early each day would be enough.

That afternoon, Lisette got ready to leave at about three thirty. Sandra insisted that Lisette skip some clean-up duties so she could get out of there sooner.

"The goal is for you to leave early so you can relax," she would say in a friendly but stern manner.

The air was dry for August in Baltimore and a gentle cool breeze hit Lisette's arms and legs as she stepped through the glass doors in the front of the diner. She breathed in some of the fresh air and headed in the direction of the Inner Harbor. The feel of the air gave Lisette confidence that her feet could handle a little extra walking.

She passed Uncle Lee's, the Chinese restaurant near Bob's Diner, and crossed Lombard Street. Her walk nowadays was a full-fledged waddle and much slower. She didn't want to trip on any cracks or debris in the sidewalk. So, she slowly plodded along, often looking downward.

When Lisette was close to the corner of the Brookshire Hotel, a man in a dark suit seemed to appear out of nowhere and wasn't dodging around her. In his hurry, he seemed to be about to plow right through her. Lisette held her arms straight out to protect the baby. In a last-minute realization, the man's arms straightened as well and grabbed hold of Lisette's shoulders to prevent the collision. Somehow both stayed on their feet.

Long, deep sighs escaped both of their lips. Lisette looked up at the man, embarrassed from not paying enough attention. That's when she noticed it was David.

David broke out in a broad smile. "Lisette, how are you?"

"Umm...I'm...I'm good," she squeaked out.

"I didn't mean to startle you. I guess I wasn't paying enough attention." David apologized.

"Me neither." Lisette's eyes diverted to a gum wrapper on the sidewalk to avoid the gaze of his brown eyes. If she had to run into someone why did it have to be him?

"I'm definitely glad I didn't knock you down or anything. Then my klutziness could have hurt you and the baby." David chuckled to lighten the mood.

Lisette looked up in time to see that twinkle in his eyes when he laughed but looked away as soon as she saw it. Why did she have to notice things like that? She had no right.

"Lisette, are you sure you're okay? You look a little dazed."

"I'm okay," she said, "But...I've got to go." She tried to walk around David.

He stepped in front of her. "Lisette, I'm sorry for almost knocking you over. But is there something else wrong?"

"No, there's nothing wrong. But I've got to go." Lisette shoved at David's arm to get around him.

David looked bewildered but didn't stop her. She moved as quickly as her legs could go, which wasn't very fast.

Lisette tripped on an uneven sidewalk and fell toward the ground. Panic ran through her as she turned her body so that when she landed, she'd be on her side instead of her stomach. However, two arms grabbed her before she hit the ground. David swooped her into his arms and carried her to the nearest bench.

He laid her down and then kneeled in front of her. "Are you okay? Does anything hurt? Is the baby okay?" He was breathing so hard that it seemed like he was the one who had fallen.

"I...I think so...I don't hurt anywhere." Her voice sounded more shaken up than if she had completed her fall. "Thanks to you, I don't think I even touched the ground."

David reached for Lisette's hand to calm her and breathed in and out to calm his own breathing. "You didn't."

"Thank you." Lisette said again.

She laid there in a daze without moving a muscle for quite a few minutes. The cool air seemed even cooler on her flushed face. Her mind was racing with thoughts of losing the baby. Roger's baby. Lisette couldn't have that. She didn't feel like anything was wrong with the baby, but she was still nervous. Even if she hadn't hit the ground, what if all her worry and anxiety had harmed the baby? "What if" ideas flooded her mind. All she could hear on the busy downtown street corner was her own worries and frets. She willed herself to be more careful.

If she hadn't been in such a hurry to get away from David, it wouldn't have happened. Why did she have to run into him this afternoon? If she hadn't, none of this would have happened. Why did she take a walk after work? Why hadn't she gone straight home?

It seemed like hours when Lisette finally heard voices walking by and traffic moving down the street again, but she was sure it was only a few minutes. When she remembered that she was lying on a bench outside and David's hand was holding her hand, she jerked her hand away as she shot up into a sitting position. "I've got to go."

David appeared stunned at her sudden outburst. "Are you okay?"

"Yes, I'm okay but I've really got to go."

"Lisette, I'm not going to hurt you. It's David. I thought we were friends."

"We can't be friends," she pled.

"Why not?" David took a breath and then spoke slower and calmer. "Why can't we be friends? I know. I'm sorry I haven't been around lately. But...your friend thought maybe I was causing more problems for you."

"You are." Lisette burst into a flood of tears and buried her face in her hands. Loud sobs of intense pain came out of her and she knew people on the street were staring.

Lisette's sudden outburst shocked David even more. He leaned closer and then stood up from his kneeling position and sat down on the bench next to her. His hand reached around her and rubbed her back gently. She peeked through her fingers and notice that every person that walked by them was looking at them. But who could blame them? It must have been quite a spectacle. This caused Lisette to hide her face in her hands again. She covered her eyes again with her hands like a little child that thinks if he covers his eyes no one can see him.

Her sobs quieted down but tears still slipped down her cheeks. Her index fingers rubbed at her eyes to dry them. David continued to sit beside Lisette while rubbing her back in slow circles with the palm of his hand. When there were no more tears left to cry. Lisette's eyes were parched and raw. She sat up straight and turned to look at David. David removed his hand from her back quickly as if she might scold him.

Lisette locked into those brown eyes of his and saw only kindness. This man just wanted to help her, and she was being rotten to him. "I...I'm sorry."

The corners of David's mouth curved into a slight smile. "Why are you sorry?"

"I...I'm horrible. You...you just want to be nice and be my friend. You even bought me a present."

"You're not horrible, Lisette, I never thought that." David paused as he looked deep into her eyes. "You've been through an awful lot."

"That's no excuse. I should be stronger."

"You are strong, Lisette. You're working your butt off for this baby." David pointed to her belly. "And it will be proud to call you its mom."

"What if I can't do it?"

"You can."

She tried to grin to show her thankfulness for his help.

David smiled back. There didn't seem to be a dishonest bone in David's body. "You'll be okay, and I'll be here to make sure you are."

It felt good to have a man by her side again, offering to help her.

CHAPTER 10

The pungent, clean smell of antiseptic hit Lisette as she walked into the waiting room of her doctor's office. She was just there for a regular check-up, but she was glad it had been scheduled for today after her almost fall. Hopefully, she hadn't harmed the baby. She signed in and then took a seat in one of the dark blue padded chairs.

A few moments later, the door to the exam rooms opened and the brunette nurse that had greeted Lisette at most of her appointments called her name. Lisette got up and walked toward her.

"It looks like this will be your last appointment before the big event, Lisette, are you ready?" The nurse spoke with excitement in her voice.

Lisette gave the nurse a half grin. She wished that she could be that excited.

The nurse looked confused but nodded and then escorted Lisette into the exam room. Lisette stole a glance at the nurse's name tag. Lisette didn't want to make it obvious that she couldn't remember her name. *Judy*, Lisette read.

Judy got the room ready for the check-up and then stayed in the room to chaperon the procedure. Lisette remembered that she usually took it a step further and held onto her hand.

The doctor came in and asked her how she was doing. Lisette smiled and nodded so he got right to his work. The cold goo squirted onto Lisette's protruding belly. She didn't know the name of that gooey stuff, but she wished that they could microwave it for a few seconds beforehand. When her belly was shiny and cold, the doctor slid the Doppler around until he picked up a quick heartbeat. Lisette could hear it on the speaker, but it seemed too fast. She frowned. The doctor smiled and said, "It's good, Lisette. The baby seems to be strong and healthy."

A sigh escaped Lisette's lips, but she also cringed as she heard the word baby. She was happy that the baby seemed all right after yesterday, but anxious thoughts always seemed to control her. Lisette still couldn't believe she would have one and she didn't even know if she'd be able to keep it. It always felt like too much.

As she focused on the sonogram picture on the screen, a wave of heat came over her. There's a real baby in her belly. She tried to concentrate as her doctor pointed to the screen. The little baby lied curled up but moved its hands and feet as if it was trying to get their attention. Lisette stared at the little thing that looked so comfortable inside her and wondered if it would feel as comfortable in a few weeks when it was outside and saw she was all it had.

"Are you sure you don't want to know the sex of the baby beforehand? Do you have questions about the birthing process? We're in the home stretch now." Dr. Berger ran his sentences together as if he was in a hurry and Lisette didn't know if he wanted an answer, but she gave one anyway.

"I guess I want to be surprised after the delivery but is there anything I can do about my feet and ankles swelling up so much? They are uncomfortable and I'm not sleeping well. No position is comfortable," Lisette complained.

Dr. Berger grinned. "Those symptoms are just par for the course. Just elevate your feet as much as you can and use a lot of pillows at night all around you." Then he patted her shoulder. "Those symptoms will be over soon."

Lisette sighed again and thought, *but then there will be even more problems.*

The doctor grinned once again and continued. "But, again, you are in the home stretch. August 20th is just around the corner. You can make it."

Her doctor had decided that it would be best for her to have a C-section because in previous visits the baby's heartbeat seemed a little slow even though that day it seemed fine. He had assured her it was only a precaution, and the baby seemed like a healthy one. Lisette was glad she wouldn't have to feel most of the procedure. She wished that she could sleep through it.

Lisette took the bus from the doctor's office to her

apartment building, walked the half a block from the bus stop to the building, and then headed straight up to her apartment so she could put her feet up. Doctor's orders. As the elevator moved upward, she placed both hands on her rounded belly and again wondered what it would be like when this little one arrived.

Would she know what to do? Was she prepared to care for a baby twenty-four-seven? She had been reading her copy of *What to Expect the First Year* that Sandra bought her as a gift but there was a lot to learn. She hoped that some of it would come naturally. After all, babies were born and cared for long before books like that existed. Still, the book was chocked full of many tips and Lisette assumed it might help her.

It's always good to be prepared, Lisette heard Roger's voice within her head as she turned the key in her front door lock. Roger knew what to do most of the time. She had always relied on his knowledge and foresight.

She hurried to close the door behind her. When Lisette was alone in her living room, she cried aloud, "Oh Roger, I'm trying to be prepared. I really am but I don't think I can do this without you."

The competent voice of Roger rang again in Lisette's head, *You will be okay, Sweetie. You're smart and you can handle more than you think you can.* He had spoken those words to her many times while they were both studying for final exams. She had always worried too much before exams even though she ended up doing just fine on them. She hoped that would be the case when the baby came.

Again, she heard Roger's voice in her head. *When you feel all anxious inside, pull out a piece of notebook paper and write your feelings. Lisette, you write well. All your papers are A-quality work. You should use that ability to work through your thoughts and feelings. You might feel less anxiety.* Lisette had forgotten that Roger had told her that during their senior year of college. That sounded a lot like David's advice a few weeks ago.

Feeling inspired, Lisette got up and walked into her bedroom to the nightstand and opened the drawer to retrieve the fuchsia blank book and pen. She brought it back to her place in the living room and propped up her feet again on the ottoman. She crossed off the date she had written when she first got the book and underneath wrote the current date. Then she wrote the first entry in her new journal:

In two weeks, you'll be here, Little One. I'm both excited and scared. I want to meet you but I'm afraid I'll mess something up. Your dad would have known what to do most of the time. I wish you could have met him. He would have been a great father to you. I loved your dad so much and I still miss him every day.

Lisette didn't know why she wrote as if she was writing to her unborn child but decide that maybe it was a good thing. She dedicated the journal to this child.

But what if she gave it up for adoption? Would the words she'd write in there be wasted?

She flipped back to the inside front cover where David had written, *Just for you.*

She guessed that anything she wrote could help her cope no matter what else happened.

CHAPTER 11

David was back in the diner again for lunch and this time Lisette was glad. He was *just a friend*, and it seemed like he'd be a good one. She greeted him with a friendly smile. Sandra did too. Sandra probably hoped that David and Lisette would eventually get together, but Lisette knew they were just friends and that would never happen.

David seemed a little taken back by the overzealous greetings. However, after saying hello, he got right to his order. "I think I'll have the grilled cheese and tomato soup, Lisette. Comfort food will taste wonderful. It's been a stressful week at work and I'm glad it's Friday."

"Coke or coffee with that?" Lisette asked.

"Coke."

She jotted his order down and took it to the kitchen to place it. Then she filled a plastic glass with ice and soda and took it back to his table. Before his food was ready, Lisette took a couple more orders. A few moments later, she brought David's food to him.

David looked up at her, smiled, and said a very warm, "Thank you."

There was that gaze that seemed to look right through her again. She blushed and replied, "You're welcome," before she turned away from him. Why did she always seem to blush when David was around? Lisette wished she could stop. It was very inappropriate.

A few moments later, she remembered something and headed back over to his table. She took a quick breath of courage and then spoke. "Oh, David, I wrote my first entry in that journal book."

"That's great, Lisette, I hope it really helps you to get some of your thoughts down on paper."

Lisette turned to move away from his table. David interjected, "Oh," as if he remembered something. He reached into his shirt pocket and pulled out a small square white envelope which he handed to Lisette. "This is for you."

"Me?" Lisette knew her confusion must have shown on her face.

"I thought you deserved a little treat. You've only got about two weeks before your blessed event."

"But you didn't have to get me anything. David...why?"

David placed his right index finger toward his lips. "Shh, I wanted to. We're friends remember? Friends can do these types of things."

Lisette shook her head and against her better judgment opened the envelope. She pulled out a little white card that appeared to be an invitation. It said,

Maximizing You with an address under it that Lisette recognized as a little salon two blocks away. Under the address, it read: *You are invited to a prenatal massage and a pedicure. Just show this card as payment for your services.*

Lisette had never had a massage and was excited at the possibility, especially when her lower back and feet ached so much. It was the perfect gift.

David seemed to appreciate the wide smile on Lisette's face as she finished reading the card.

She wanted to repeat to him he didn't have to do such a thing for her but only the words, "Thank you," escaped Lisette's lips.

She redeemed the coupon that evening. She always passed Maximizing You on her way home from work, so she asked if they had an opening. The decor was done with serene blues and mystic purples that made for a soothing atmosphere. The receptionist announced that they had an opening, so Lisette entered pure bliss for almost two hours. The massage soothed her aching back and the pedicure revived her tired feet. Soothing music over the salon's intercom system caused Lisette's mind to clear of some of its worries. She walked on air the rest of the way to her apartment.

When she got home, she took out her journal.

I want you to know, although bad things happen in the world you're about to be born in, good things also happen. People can be very nice and kind. One day I'll tell you about the bad thing that happened to your daddy but until the time is right, I hope you have so many good memories built up it will provide a cushion for the bad ones to land on.

The following Monday, when David paid his lunch bill, he handed Lisette a twenty-five-dollar gift card for Baby Time, a baby store that was just a few blocks away. She shook her head no and refused to accept the gift, but he wouldn't have it.

"I wanted to do something nice for the baby, that's all," he insisted. Lisette gave up her resistance and thanked him, but she wondered again why he was being so nice.

On Tuesday, he gave her another twenty-five-dollar gift card for the downtown grocery store. This time, Lisette didn't say no but she was glad he couldn't hear her thoughts. On the outside, she said a polite "Thank you" but on the inside, she was wondering what was going on.

Wednesday, David offered her a twenty-five-dollar gift card for a women's clothing store to help her get something non-maternity after she gave birth. This time, Lisette smiled through slightly clenched teeth. What was he trying to accomplish? However, she still said thank you while reminding herself that he was just being nice. But she was wondering if he thought she was some huge charity case. Was he trying to get a merit badge or something?

On Thursday, he gave her another twenty-five-dollar grocery store gift card.

Lisette felt like she had to continue to be polite. Customers were all around her. She again voiced the words thank you, but a smile didn't accompany her words this time. What was his deal? Was he a knight in shining armor in a previous life? Did he want her to feel like she owed him, so she'd go out with him? What was his ulterior motive? There had to be one.

On Friday, at lunchtime, David handed Lisette yet another white envelope with her name printed on it. Her first thought was to hand it back to him unopened and tell him that enough is enough. But she swallowed that first idea reluctantly and instead opened the envelope. Her lips pressed together as if they were trying to hold back the flood of words that wanted to escape them. Words that might not be so nice.

When she looked inside the envelope, there was another gift card for Baby Time and this one was for fifty dollars.

Something took over Lisette as she shook the card in front of David's face and asked him, "What are you doing?" She was not smiling. She was downright mad at his audacity. She didn't need his charity. She could take care of herself just fine.

David stiffened and jerked back in his seat as if Lisette had smacked him across his face instead of just creating a breeze in front of it.

"I...I was just trying to be nice."

"There is such a thing as being too nice, David." Lisette shook her head. "Nobody is this nice. It's creepy when people are this nice." She noticed customers watching her outburst, but she didn't care.

"I...I just wanted..."

Lisette interrupted his stammer. "Let me rephrase that. Nobody is this nice without an ulterior motive." She gathered her thoughts. She felt like a volcano had just erupted in her head. "What is your motive, David? What do you want from me?" Before David responded, Lisette continued. "Am I a big charity case to you? So you can feel good that you helped the poor young widow?"

"Well, I really did just want to be nice." David looked down at his feet. "I know you're not a charity case, Lisette. But you mentioned that money would be tight after the baby came."

"I can take care of myself. I've been doing fine so far, without your help. I don't need all of this." She waved the card in front of his face again.

"I know you can, Lisette." David's voice was the opposite of mine. He stayed calm even amid Hurricane Lisette. "I thought you've had a rough year and maybe you could use some kindness. I wanted to be your friend."

"What else do you want, David? Tell me." Lisette didn't think she'd ever been this demanding in her whole life, but she didn't care what she sounded like right then. She wanted to get to the truth of the situation.

David looked directly at Lisette with those warm brown eyes. "I guess I had an extra motive."

"What?" Lisette scared herself with the abruptness of her own voice.

"Well, on the surface, I really did just want to bring you some happiness and to be your friend. That's all. Really. But, I guess also, I hoped that one day...maybe you'd go out with me again." He paused before he added, "But only if you're ready. I would never want to push you into anything."

Lisette's voice calmed down after seeing the genuine-looking empathy in his eyes. She knew David cared. But she still added, "Spending all kinds of money on me isn't pushing?"

"I guess I didn't think that part through. I sometimes do spontaneous things, but I never meant to push you. When we had dinner, I remembered you saying how you were trying to save almost every penny for after the baby comes. I guess I thought these gifts would help. I didn't think...that's all." David's mouth formed a squeamish smile, but his eyes fixated on Lisette. Eyes that looked as if they were truly sorry.

"I realize that you want to be more than friends, David. But I can't offer you that. Not now and I don't think ever. I don't see you that way, David." Lisette left out the part that she saw no man that way anymore.

David again looked as if Lisette had smacked him. She didn't want to hurt him, but she couldn't let this go on either. She looked down at her white tennis shoes as she continued. "There's no future for us, David. If you want to come in for lunch, please sit in Sandra's station. It'll be easier on everyone." Lisette turned away and headed for the solace of the kitchen.

At home, that night she again wrote in her journal. She tried to forget where it came from even though she couldn't. Lisette would always remember the nice man who gave it to her.

Baby, I want to let you know people can be very nice. In addition, some people have an extra helping gene or something. I've met a person like that. Someone who went out of their way to help me. You won't meet him though. Today, I made sure of that. But for now, I want to tell you that nice people exist even though you have to think about their motives for being nice. Try not to be cynical when bad things happen in this world. Try to remember the good.

A good quality night's sleep didn't come. Lisette managed a few scattered bouts of sleep, but they were so scattered that rest did not accompany them. Visions of a hurting David wouldn't leave her mind. Roger showed up confirming she was right about her conclusions. And, there were the same old worries of not being able to take care of her baby haunting her. No wonder she couldn't sleep.

At four o'clock, Lisette gave up and took her shower. She would be very early for work. Maybe fresh morning air would do her some good. She walked down Pratt Street because it seems to be the most lit up in the wee hours of the morning. Sarah's Donut Shoppe with its bright pink neon lighting and fuchsia awning was like a beacon to Lisette's tired, bloodshot eyes. She ordered a cinnamon sugar donut and a carton of milk. The sugar might help to wake her up. She paid for her breakfast and slipped both into her purse. She'd have breakfast when she was closer to work.

She continued onward in the diner's direction until she got to the TransAmerica building. She walked up the concrete stairs and found an empty black metal bench that faced the harbor area. As Lisette sat down, she noticed that the sun was making a pinkish line at the horizon over the east side of the harbor. Maybe a sunrise would make up for not sleeping well.

She took out her breakfast items, unfolded the white paper napkin, and laid it on the top of her belly. Then she took out her cinnamon donut and un-wrapped it from its wax paper covering. It was still warm and the first bite melted in her mouth. She opened the carton of milk and took a swig of the cold, creamy liquid, which cleansed her palate. A few bites of the donut made it disappear.

Lisette dusted the cinnamon sugar dust off her stomach and used the napkin to wipe her mouth. She picked up the carton of milk again to finish it. A flut-tery movement came over her belly. She wondered if the baby would enjoy the nutrients from the milk. If it's like its mommy, it would also love the cinnamon sugar. Not as nutritious, but so delicious.

Lisette looked up in time to see a beautiful pink haze forming in the sky. She smiled as if she had just received a treasure. The pink slowly raised in the sky as yellow-orange took its place underneath. Then a few moments later, there was a streak of red-orange right at the horizon. The beauty of all three colors mesmerized her and she couldn't look away. It was that beautiful.

A memory of Roger and her watching another beautiful sunrise before college one day came to Lisette's mind.

"The dark buildings contrasting with those brilliant colors is intense. It makes me think God is giving us a present this morning." Roger took hold of her hand as he spoke.

"Maybe he is saying that test I have today will turn out okay." Lisette had replied.

"It will, Lisette, you're smarter and more capable than you think you are. Always remember that."

Roger was always encouraging her like that. She smiled a bittersweet smile because she was wishing that Roger was there right then to enjoy another sunrise with her. She also wished that he was there to encourage her.

The colors faded as the sunrise concluded. She got up, dropped her trash in the nearby receptacle, and continued her walk. As she turned down the street that the diner was on, she looked over and noticed the bench where David had sat with her after her almost fall. A lump appeared in her throat.

In a parallel universe where Roger's memory didn't exist and there weren't any complications, Lisette could see herself dating David. But there were a lot of complications. So, she must stick with her decision. It was a good one and the only way to honor Roger's memory.

She cleared her throat, turned her head away from that bench, and continued to walk toward the diner.

She walked by a parking garage and when she looked inside to make sure that no car was exiting, she saw David walking out. His gaze caught hers immediately. There was no hiding or even pretending she hadn't seen him. He was right there, and he was stepping closer.

"Umm...I was just...umm...going into work." He looked at her but there wasn't a sparkle in his eyes like before. He added with an apologetic tone, "Don't worry, Lisette, I'm not going into the diner."

Why did it have to be this hard? Why couldn't she simply not see him again? She didn't know if she could get any words to come out of her mouth because that lump was still in her throat. Somehow, she managed to say, "David...I'm...I'm sorry."

"You don't need to be sorry, Lisette." He forced a smile. "It's me that pushed you. I...I should have known. You had every right to stop me."

Lisette felt just awful. It wasn't David's fault she was such a mess. Any other girl would have handled this whole thing much better than her. She didn't know what they would have done but she knew it would have been a better response than hers. She looked down at the ground and wanted to disappear.

David reached out and lifted her chin with his index finger. She was forced to look up at his face.

"Hey, Lisette, this is not your fault at all. This is all on me." David's voice seemed to get stronger as he spoke. "I pushed. I messed up. You didn't do anything wrong."

"But David...you didn't mean too...I didn't handle the situation well at all."

"No...I won't hear any of that, Lisette. I put you in a terrible position and you defended yourself. That's all. I don't want to keep putting you in those situations, Lisette." David smiled warmly before continuing. "You deserve better."

If he only knew, he wouldn't be saying she deserved better. She breathed in a blast of cool morning air which seemed to energize her. "David, I liked us being friends. I really did. I...I...I can't give you more than that."

"I understand but I still need to stay away for a while. My presence isn't helping you, Lisette. It's hurting you. And I never wanted that."

"Oh," was the only response that came to Lisette's mind.

"But we are friends, Lisette. And friends do what they need to do to help the other one."

"You can come in to the diner any time, David. I'll learn to handle it better. I wish I was better at troubling situations but I'm not. I can't even guarantee I won't treat you badly again."

"You're more capable than you think you are, Lisette."

David's encouragement echoed what Roger had always told her. It seemed as if Roger was there with them and oddly that comforted her.

David walked with her the rest of the way to the

diner. She asked him if he wanted to come inside for a coffee or something.

He smiled but shook his head. Then he added, "But I will come back again, Lisette." Then he questioned, "Friends?"

Lisette nodded and repeated, "Friends." Then she watched him look both ways and then cross the street toward his office as she wondered again if she'd ever see him again. It would be easier if she didn't see him again. She felt a hollow place in her stomach. Did she want to never see him again?

CHAPTER 12

One afternoon at four o'clock, instead of going home right away, Lisette stayed in the diner to talk with Sandra while Sandra worked.

Lisette wanted to get more of Sandra's opinion on the whole David issue. Lisette thought she knew what Sandra would say. She'd tell Lisette to *go for it.* But Lisette wanted to hear more than that. Lisette also wanted to convince Sandra of her own way of thinking.

There were only two tables of customers and one of them was ready to pay the check. So, Lisette and Sandra were able to have a good chat.

"On one hand, Sandra," Lisette began, "I see this David as a great guy. He's extremely nice and I would even consider him cute." An unconscious giggle escaped Lisette's lips which she didn't like. She was a pregnant widow. And she didn't want to have those wide-eyed feelings for anyone but Roger.

Sandra interrupted Lisette's thoughts. "Well, then, what's the problem?"

Lisette looked down at her belly and paused for a long moment.

Sandra walked closer to her, poised to listen.

"This is Roger's." Lisette pointed to herself and looked up with moist eyes.

"Honey, I know. You feel you're cheating on Roger, right?"

"Well, no, not exactly...but yes, I feel that way." Lisette stammered. "I know it makes little sense but..."

Sandra gave her a closed-mouth smile.

"I mean, I know I'm not cheating but it doesn't feel right to think about anyone but Roger. I don't think he'd want me to."

"You were with Roger for a long time, Lisette. It's only natural. And...you're still grieving," Sandra handed me a napkin.

Lisette took it and dabbed at her eyes. "So, you're saying I should date David?"

Sandra shook her head. "No, I'm not saying that."

Lisette considered her friend's large, dark brown eyes that had listened to Lisette's predicament repeatedly and seemed to care every single time. "You're saying it's my decision? Right?"

Sandra nodded while smiling that same closed-mouth smile, "No one else can make this decision for you, Lisette." Then she gave a throaty chuckle, "I know I'm great and all but even I can't do that."

"But I don't know. I don't know what to do. My mind is blank and I'm tired of thinking about David. Maybe that's a good thing? Maybe that means I should be true to Roger?" Lisette wanted Sandra to agree with her. She wanted her to tell her to stay true to Roger. If it was Lisette's decision like Sandra just said, then Sandra should let her stay true to Roger and not date anyone else. Right?

"Lisette, your feelings of guilt are understandable and even normal. But that doesn't mean they're valid." Sandra stopped wiping a table, came closer, and squeezed Lisette's shoulder with her right hand.

"That makes no sense, Sandra. Why aren't my feelings valid? Just because Roger died? That doesn't mean we didn't have something special."

"You had something special. From what you've shared with me, I know that you and Roger had a great romance. I'm even jealous of your memories. However, your vows were 'til death do us part only, not necessarily after." Sandra paused long enough to clear her throat before continuing. "I think some people might be called to not date ever again after a spouse dies. If you feel that's what you're supposed to do, that's fine. I'll back you up all the way."

Lisette opened her mouth to respond because that's what she wanted to hear her friend say.

Sandra interjected. "But...there are extenuating circumstances in your case. That little baby is a big extenuating circumstance. And...God just might bring you someone to help you. And you deserve that, Lisette."

Sandra paused. Lisette tried to swallow Sandra's words but they caught in her throat.

"Lisette, I know that Roger would want you and the baby to be happy." She leaned toward Lisette and wrapped her arms around her. "I know you'll do the right thing, And, no matter what you decide, I'll be here to help you."

Lisette's jumbled mind made her walk home from work seem extra-long. She could have absent-mindedly stepped right off the curb and into traffic. If she did, David could step out of nowhere and swoop her up to safety again, just like Superman. Lisette snickered at her joke which cleared some tension.

In her apartment, she picked up her journal and pen. Nibbling on the top of the pen, she wondered why she had decorated this apartment in various shades of blue and purple. It seemed right last year because she had always loved purple but now it only added to her melancholy. She would have to live with it for now though because she wasn't in any condition to paint.

Dear Baby, I know you will need a father figure in your life and that thought makes me want to date again so there's a chance for you to have one. However, I loved your real father so very much. So much that I cannot fathom having those feelings for another man.

Your father was one of a kind. Another man may be nice and even cute, but he will not be Roger. These kinds of thoughts make me consider placing you into an adoptive home. Then you would have a father to help raise you and a mother who isn't sad all the time. You deserve that.

Your father was wonderful. We dated throughout high

school and college and got married right after college. He had a way of filling in my empty places. He could also make me laugh. I know he would have made you laugh too. Often, he would make this Donald Duck type voice and call himself Super Duck. It was so whimsical and fun. It never failed to make me smile. I can see him leaning over your crib, looking down on you and making those funny sounds. Your father would have been a wonderful daddy for you.

Lisette got to the end of the journal entry when it dawned on her she didn't have a crib yet. How could she have forgotten something so important? Maybe she should give the baby up for adoption if she could forget something that important. Lisette rolled her eyes at her forgetfulness.

She took a deep breath and noticed that it was only a little after six o'clock. Maybe she could get a crib to-night? But she didn't have a car and she couldn't get a crib onto the bus.

Lisette flipped the pages in her journal and it fell open to the inside front cover.

Not knowing what else to do, she picked up the fuchsia journal book and looked closer at the phone number David had written. Lisette didn't want to call him, but she felt like she had no other option. She wished she had more friends around here, especially some that owned a car.

Lisette picked up her phone and dialed that num-ber, the same number she had vowed never to call. Lisette would clarify she only wanted a ride to Baby Time.

After the fourth ring Lisette heard, "Hello."

David's soothing, familiar voice came through the phone speaker.

Lisette placed the phone back up toward her face. "Hi...umm...David?" she asked.

"Lisette? Is that you? Is everything okay?"

"I'm fine, but David I remembered that I don't have a crib. I know. I should have gotten one by now. I don't know how it could have slipped my mind. But...I don't have one. And I don't have a car to pick one up with." Guilt overcame her for forgetting something so vital and for asking David for this huge favor.

David interrupted her and said, "I can come pick you up now. Baby Time will be open a few more hours. Do you like that store?"

"Yes, Baby Time is a good store." A smile of gratitude came across Lisette's face. He knew what she wanted without her even asking. There weren't many people that would drop what they were doing at a moment's notice to help a stranger. "Umm...I'm ready now. I can wait outside my apartment building. Oh...and David?"

"What?"

She didn't want to let this extreme burden go by without an acknowledgment. "Thank you."

"No problem."

Lisette pressed the end call button and then laughed aloud as she thought of her joke from before. David would drop everything to help a damsel in distress. Maybe he was Superman.

Lisette's eye caught a beautiful, antique white crib as soon as she entered Baby Time. She made a beeline for it immediately. As she got closer, she noticed the simple design, but it was elegant in its simplicity. However, she didn't like the cost which was a little over three hundred dollars, so she walked down the aisle looking at the price tags of the other models.

A lot of them were even more expensive. A few of them were a little less. Lisette kept looking back at the first one. On the plus side, the first one could convert into a toddler bed later, so it would save money in the long run. That was enough to convince her the first one was the one.

The bed didn't come with bedding, so she also had to get a mattress, sheet, and bumper pads. Lisette had read that a small amount of bedding was best. Everything was on sale, but the total bill was still over four hundred dollars. Lisette used the two gift cards that David had given her and sighed as she slid her credit card through the machine to pay for the rest. This was only the beginning, she thought. Her expenses would only grow larger.

David carried and loaded everything into his car. Lisette just had to load herself into the front seat.

David walked over to the passenger side. "I'll be right back." Then he walked back into the store.

In about five minutes, he was back with a multicolored Baby Time plastic bag dangling from his arm. He walked to the car door on Lisette's side. She rolled down the window wondering if something was wrong.

He bent over and reached the plastic bag through the window. As he did, Lisette noticed the V of his polo shirt. She couldn't see any chest hair and contrasted it to Roger's dark, curly chest hair. A warmth of embarrassment crept into Lisette's cheeks for noticing that detail.

"I wanted to get the baby a present." David added, "It's for the baby, not another one for you."

The bag landed between Lisette's large stomach and the car door. Then David went around to the other side of the car and slipped into the driver's seat.

"You didn't have to do that, David, really." She responded, still uncomfortable with David's generosity towards her.

"No, I didn't have to. I wanted to." He smiled.

Lisette still hadn't taken hold of the bag. It had dropped between her and the door.

David looked over and smiled again. "You can open it. You don't have to wait until the baby's born."

Another warmth crept into her cheeks as she dutifully moved the bag into a position in which she could open it. However, this warmth didn't seem to be from embarrassment. Could it be happiness? But happiness had eluded her for a long time.

Lisette reached into the bag and pulled out a super-soft light brown teddy bear. The tag said it played in three modes: mommy's womb sounds, three lullabies, and two nature sounds. Lisette looked up at

David, her eyes moist. "Thank you, David." Then she hugged the teddy bear to her belly. "I'm sure that the baby loves it already."

"You're welcome. It's my pleasure."

A joy radiated from David at that moment that made Lisette smile.

When they arrived back at her apartment building, David carried the crib box and accessories up. Then he promised to come back the next evening to put it together for her. She was again grateful since Roger had always done things like that.

When David left, Lisette settled onto her couch with her swollen feet propped up. She turned on the lullaby sounds and laid the teddy bear across her rounded belly. Maybe the baby would hear the peaceful songs.

Then Lisette picked up her journal book and pen.

You received your first present, Little One. A cute little brown teddy bear that plays peaceful sounds. Can you hear it? I'm playing it for you right now. It came from a very nice friend of mine. Even if I end up giving you up for adoption, I hope you will always keep this special little teddy bear wherever you end up.

Lisette nibbled on the top of the pen. The more she thought about all the expenses involved with raising a baby, the more she was leaning toward adoption.

CHAPTER 13

The next evening, as promised, David came back to Lisette's apartment to put the crib together. Earlier in the day, Lisette had called him and attempted to get him to renege on his offer. Lisette didn't want to take advantage of him like that again. In typical David style, he insisted that it wasn't an imposition and that he wanted to help.

The practical side of her was glad that David didn't listen to her. She needed help with the crib. So, to apply salve to her bruised ego, she told him she would fix him dinner while he was assembling the crib.

While David worked, Lisette prepared dinner. She broiled steaks, baked potatoes, and steamed broccoli. It had been a long time since she'd cooked a meal in her kitchen. She was indebted to David for all his help. It was the least she could do.

At around seven thirty, David announced that he was done so Lisette waddled into her bedroom to see the beautifully constructed crib. When she saw the crib sitting underneath the window, she smiled.

It was where she had planned to put it, except she hadn't told David that. He just knew. He had even made up the little bed with the new bedding, so it looked like the store display. The teddy bear he had bought the baby was sitting up inside the crib as well. Another large smile beamed across Lisette's face. To which David smiled back, pleased by her reaction.

The timer for the potatoes dinged and brought Lisette out of her dreamy state. "Well this is great timing. Dinner's ready too."

They both went down the short hallway. David darted into the bathroom to wash his hands and Lisette got all the food to the table.

David sat down at the table. "Everything smells great, Lisette."

"Thank you." She sat down at the table too.

"No...thank you." David winked his usual wink.

Lisette tried to hide the excitement that bubbled up inside her when she looked at David by stuffing a piece of broccoli in her mouth. It was an excitement that shouldn't be there.

"Do you mind if I say grace, Lisette?"

Embarrassed, Lisette swallowed the broccoli and took a sip of water to ease the sudden gulp. Then she said, "No, I don't mind."

David spoke a simple prayer of gratitude while Lisette's mind wandered. Roger and she used to pray a lot. Why had she stopped? Lisette shook her head to answer herself as David spoke the word, "Amen." She remembered why she had stopped praying. It was in November when God stopped caring about her.

They were both hungry, so they ate without a lot of small talk. David was a very nice man, but Lisette couldn't get over how uncomfortable she was around him.

When both plates were empty, David got up first and picked them both up.

"You don't have to do that. Put those down." Lisette attempted to order him.

"No. No." David smiled as he continued walking the plates to the sink.

Lisette followed him with the glasses in her hand.

David loaded everything into the dishwasher and they both went into the living room. However, Lisette didn't sit down.

David said, "I won't stay much longer, Lisette. I know you have to get up for work tomorrow morning and so do I."

Lisette was relieved to hear him say that, but she politely said, "But sit for a few minutes, David." She wanted him to leave but she couldn't be rude. He put together the entire crib for her. Not to mention all the many other ways he had helped her.

David sat down on the dark blue armchair. Not wanting to get too close, Lisette sat on the matching couch, across the room.

"Okay, but I really won't stay long. You need your rest," he insisted again.

Lisette swallowed a couple times and then bit the corner of her lip before she spoke. She wanted an opportunity like this to straighten things out with him once and for all. Clear up any misunderstandings. Maybe she could finally learn just why he was so very nice to her. "Well...umm...I'm very grateful for all you've done for me, David. I really am."

"But?"

"It's just that...umm..."

David pursed his lips as he waited.

Lisette paused and took a deep breath and just came right out with it. "David, I guess I want to ask you why. Why have you been so nice to me?"

"I guess the simple answer is what I have said before, that you seem like a very nice lady. Someone I would like to date, if circumstances were different, that is." David cleared his throat and then added, "But...being just friends is okay too."

"Under different circumstances, I probably would've dated you a few times by now," Lisette offered. "But circumstances are what they are, and I've got a lot to think about right now."

"I know. And I understand."

David's eyes always seemed to look right inside Lisette like a doctor's otoscope. Lisette found it very hard to believe David understood her like he said. How could he? She had been through an awful lot. "But David, what if I never get to the place where you are? What if I never want to date you?"

"That's the chance I'll take." David looked Lisette straight in her eyes again. "But no matter what, I will have gotten the chance to know and help you. There's nothing wrong with that, is there?"

"What's in it for you?" Lisette squinted her eyes.

"No matter what, I'll have a new friend and I am

okay with just friends. There's really nothing wrong with that," David repeated with emphasis.

Lisette saw that sparkle in his eyes she'd reluctantly grown to like very much. Why did she ever have to meet him in the first place? This was just too complicated. Lisette looked away, so she could clear her head.

"But...there is another reason I want to help you." Then David scooted backward in his seat a little more like he was getting comfortable for a long ride. "Something that helps me to feel genuine empathy about your situation."

Lisette sat up straighter, with her ears and eyes at full attention.

David swallowed hard before beginning. "I was married before, Lisette. Her name was Laura. We met during my sophomore year of college."

Lisette watched as David's mouth turned up in a slight smile. She knew that pensive look intimately because she had felt it in her many memories of Roger. She knew he was remembering this young lady fondly.

"I was pre-law and she was a business major. She could see the big picture of most situations and wanted to be a CEO of a company. She could have become one too. She was that smart and sharp." David looked more and more relaxed as he spoke of Laura. "Well, we fell in love and married right after we graduated college."

"Just like me and Roger." Now it was Lisette's turn to sigh at the memories in her head. Then she also wondered what had happened to this Laura. Had she had such high career aspirations that marriage didn't seem to fit in? Did she leave him?

David nodded. "We knew it might be difficult because I would go on to law school, but we married then anyway. Just a tiny justice of the peace ceremony but we were finally man and wife." David's smile amplified.

Lisette smiled along with him remembering her own perfect little justice of the peace ceremony.

David took another deep breath. "We didn't plan it, but Laura got pregnant during my first year of law school. It wasn't the right time at all but we both wanted to make the best of it because we loved each other. We assumed we could handle whatever we had to handle. The baby was due in the middle of my second year of law school."

David paused then, and Lisette saw that his shoulders and chin had dropped a little. She wondered again what could have happened that they weren't together still. Where was Laura now? Did she leave David and take the baby with her? How could she have done that? If Lisette still had Roger with her, she would never leave him no matter what.

He continued. "I...I think it was about the thirtieth week of her pregnancy. L...Laura went in for a regular check-up and...and her blood pressure was too high. The doctor diagnosed her with pre-eclampsia and then scheduled her for two doctor's appointments each week from then on out. He also scheduled a Caesarean section for her fortieth week."

Lisette's eyes grew big as she interrupted him. "My...my doctor scheduled me for a Caesarean section for my fortieth week. Could there be something wrong?"

"Hopefully not," David consoled. "Did you have high blood pressure?"

"No, not that I know of."

"Well, your doctor would have told you if you did." David assured me.

"Oh," Lisette relaxed a bit but was still a little worried. Worry and anxiety could cause high blood pressure and she had been worried a lot throughout this pregnancy. She made a mental note to ask her doctor about any possible complications.

"Pre-eclampsia doesn't happen in a lot of cases." David assured Lisette again. "You're probably okay or your doctor would have already diagnosed you with it."

Lisette nodded slowly. She wanted to hear more about Laura and their baby. "Okay, but please go on with your story, David."

David nodded but didn't speak right away. Instead, he stood up and paced the short distance of her living room twice. Lisette gripped the couch's arm rest and braced herself for whatever was coming next.

David spoke again from a standing position this time. "At her doctor's visits, she seemed okay. Her blood pressure was still always a little high, but it never got worse whenever it was checked. The doctor thought she would be...fine." His pronunciation of fine sounded halted and abrupt, followed by a deep, forced exhale.

Lisette leaned forward with even greater concern. Something terrible must have happened.

"The day of her Caesarean section arrived. We were in the home stretch. We had made it." David paused again. "But...but two hours before it was scheduled, Laura developed a bad headache and her blood pressure skyrocketed. I...I never saw nurses and orderlies move so fast. More people than I could count came into her room and seemed to swirl all around Laura and me. They did a lot of checking her and talking to each other and then dashed Laura on a gurney out of her room, through the halls, straight into the operating room. They didn't even have time to explain anything. I...I didn't know what to think or do. I felt helpless. So, I waited. Waited for the doctor to come out with the good news I was hoping for, at least that is what I prayed."

Lisette's mouth dropped open. "Oh no, what a terrible thing to go through." She reached for David's hand to comfort him.

David reached for her hand but before he could, his knees buckled, and he stumbled a step forward as he fell to his knees right in front of Lisette. His eyes glazed over, and his chin trembled. Then Lisette's hand reached out to touch David's shoulder. She would never have guessed that David had gone through such a tragedy. He seemed so happy-go-lucky.

David composed himself and continued with his story. "A couple hours later, the doctor came out to where I was sitting in the waiting room. His somber expression told me most of the story before he spoke. Laura and the baby both died." With that, David's neck looked like it was overburdened by the weight of the memories in his own head and it fell forward. With knees on the ground and face bowed down, David looked like he was praying, and Lisette thought she would disturb him if she said anything, so she remained quiet. Soft whimpers escaped his lips as Lisette pulled his head, so his forehead could rest on her knee as she rubbed the brown hair on the sides of his temples.

They remained like that for a few moments. David lifted his head and straightened up to a full standing position. "I'm sorry, Lisette. I didn't mean to burden you with my story."

Lisette interrupted him. "David, it wasn't a burden. Even though it was hard to hear, I wanted to hear it."

"Thank you, Lisette. I guess I had forgotten the full effect of re-telling my story. It has been a long time since I told it in such detail. The memories became fresh again."

Lisette nodded, knowing what David meant.

"Even though I have been able to go on with my life to the best of my ability, I don't think I'll ever completely get over what happened. Actually, I don't think anybody should completely get over tragedies like that," David theorized.

Lisette squinted a little to understand what he was saying.

He continued. "I mean that although it's imperative

to live again after a tragedy, it's also important to always remember what it was like to go through the tragedy, so you can help someone else in a similar situation."

Lisette nodded robotically. She believed what he said. It made perfect sense, but she guessed it was one of those things that took a while to digest.

David continued. "Well, that is why I think I can be empathetic to your plight, Lisette. I've been somewhere very similar."

Lisette nodded again. She couldn't deny that fact.

David smiled, maybe just to lighten the mood a bit, and added, "From the first moment I met you, Lisette, you reminded me of Laura. You don't really look like her but there's something about you that is like Laura. You were both kind and joyful."

Now, Lisette knew David must have lost his marbles. Her? Kind and happy? She was depressed all the time and on the verge of crying most days.

David smiled again at Lisette's obvious confusion. "Oh...I know you're sad a lot, Lisette. But underneath of all that sadness there remains something of how you used to be—before the tragedy. And...it still tries to come out whether you want it to or not."

Later that night, she wrote:

It seems like many people have a sad, even tragic, story to tell. Why do such bad things have to happen? Why can't everything be happy and idyllic all the time? Or at least average? Why do such tragedies happen? Why does God allow them? I don't expect an answer to these questions. Answers rarely come. I have always believed in some kind of God even as a child.

During high school, Roger introduced me to the God he knew from the bible. He also gave me a bible which I read regularly. Roger had great faith. I believed too. I really did. However, I guess I didn't have the confidence that Roger had. Then, after Roger died, the belief I thought I had seemed to go right out of me. Why would God do that? Why would he take my Roger away? Why would he take David's Laura and an innocent baby away from him? It's just not fair.

David's confession gave Lisette choppy sleep that night. So, she arrived at the diner a half an hour before opening the next morning. Sandra was already in the kitchen talking with Bob when Lisette first saw her. Sandra looked through the pickup window, saw Lisette, and smiled. Then she came out to the dining area.

Lisette wanted to get her take on what she had just found out about David's life and situation. However, out of respect for her and David's private conversation, she didn't tell her friend everything. It wasn't Lisette's story to tell. She wanted to tell her enough to let Sandra know David had been through his own tragedy—probably even worse than Lisette's own sad story. It almost made perfect sense why he'd been so nice to Lisette now. His other life was ripped away from him before it had begun.

Sandra shuffled condiments around as she listened to Lisette.

"Lisette, that's one of the saddest stories I've ever heard."

"I know. He lost a wife and a baby in one fell swoop."

Sandra's eyes looked up, seemingly at the corner of the ceiling. "Well, as sad as it is, it explains a lot."

Lisette looked at her friend and waited expectantly for her take on the situation.

"Don't you see, dear? Therefore, God may have brought the two of you together. You both can really understand what the other one is feeling." Sandra's bright pink mouth turned up into a satisfied smile. "I love it when I get to see some of God's plan."

Lisette's mind wandered back to testimonies she had heard when she used to attend a church. She had heard many people saying that God brought just the right thing at just the right moment. Could this be one of those cases? Does God still care for her? Even though she had not stepped into a church since last November. Yes, God had a right to be mad at her.

"Lisette, are you there?" The palm of Sandra's hand passed before Lisette's eyes and shook her out of her trance.

"I'm here. Sorry." Lisette looked down. "Do you think God would do something like that?"

"Of course, Lisette! He does stuff like that all the time. Why just last Sunday I was talking to a lady at my church and she said she was single and thirty-eight years old and just now met the man of her dreams. God loves to give good gifts to his children."

Sandra was beaming. She often got that way when she talked about God. Lisette wished she had her faith. Or the faith Roger had. Or even the faith that David seemed to have. It doesn't seem like he turned away from God even after living out a horrific tragedy.

No, God wouldn't be giving Lisette a gift because she didn't deserve one. She should have been in that car with Roger on that night. Why had she been spared?

No answer came to Lisette's mind, but Sandra's face seemed to tell a different story. Sandra had switched from beaming to downright glowing. Lisette squinted her eyes as she looked at her friend.

"Yes, God does things like that all the time, Lisette." Sandra chirped as she wiped down a table that shined after her cloth went over it. "He loves to make things new."

Sandra seemed more determined than ever that maybe David and Lisette belonged together. How could she be so sure? And yet, even Lisette had to admit that the similarity in her and David's pasts was an odd coincidence.

CHAPTER 14

I t felt strange to Lisette to go to the hospital on August 20 to have a baby when she wasn't having contractions. She guessed that was the good thing about a C-section. It happened on schedule.

She awoke early to pack what she'd need for the hospital in her overnight bag. Two nightgowns, her slippers, and warm, cuddly socks. Her feet were always cold. She added some pre-maternity clothes for going home after everything was over. Then she collected her toothbrush, toothpaste, deodorant, hair brush and comb, and lip balm. Lisette also tossed in the teddy bear that David had bought for the baby.

At eight o'clock, Lisette reached for the phone receiver to call the cab. However, before she could dial, the intercom buzzed. She stood back up again and toddled over to the front door.

"Hello?" She said as she pressed down the intercom button.

"Your ride to the hospital is here," a muffled, scratchy voice came through the speaker.

Lisette was puzzled and remained silent. She hadn't called the cab yet.

The scratchy intercom spoke again, "Lisette, It's David."

She shook her head. "I don't really have time to talk, David. I have to get to the hospital."

"I know. I came to drive you there, Lisette." David interrupted her objection.

"Why? You don't have..."

David cut her off. "Of course, I do. You can't go to the hospital to have a baby with a total stranger, even if that stranger is a cab driver." David paused but started up again before Lisette could protest. "And...I can't think of a better way to spend my birthday."

"Your birthday? Huh?" Lisette's eyebrows furrowed with confusion.

"Yes," David said. "I'll show you my driver's license later to prove it. I think that's why I remembered the day you said you would have your C-section. It's my day too."

Lisette smirked. She didn't know if he was pulling her leg or not. It was just too odd of a coincidence. But Lisette relented. "Okay, okay. I have to get to the hospital and you are here."

"Good. Come on down then. Or do you want me to come up to help you with your things?"

"Thank you but I think I'm fine. I'll be down in a minute."

Why was David always so happy to help her? A mental list ran through Lisette's head as Lisette tried to remember if she had packed everything she might need. She couldn't think of anything she had missed. Clothes, toiletries, the stuffed bear, and her journal book and pen. It was a habit to write in it now.

She picked up her overnight bag and her purse and then opened the front door. Lisette stepped into the hallway and took a deep cleansing breath. The next time she walked through that door, she wouldn't be alone. She'd have a baby with her. Lisette swallowed hard. She still couldn't imagine what it would be like to have a baby with her. And she still didn't even know if she would ultimately keep it. Maybe there wouldn't be a baby with her when she walked back in. There was still a lot to think about and to decide. She inhaled again.

When the elevator doors opened on the bottom floor, David was standing right there waiting for her.

"Thank you for getting me to the hospital, David," Lisette said. "Is it really your birthday?"

David nodded along with a tiny smile as he took hold of her bag. "Yes, and I can't think of a better way to celebrate it than with an actual birth."

David got her to the hospital in less than half an hour which meant that Lisette was early, but the nurses didn't mind at all. They began the process of admission.

"It looks like you're pre-registered, Ms. Carter, so this should only take a few."

The nurse handed Lisette a clipboard with a piece of paper on it.

"This is the consent form for your procedure."

Lisette signed.

The nurse added, "Did you bring your health insurance card and driver's license?"

Lisette nodded as she dug in her purse for her wallet. When she found it, she handed the two cards over.

"Thank you." The nurse turned around and placed both cards on the copier and made a copy "I think you're all set now." She motioned for the orderly who was already pushing a wheelchair toward them. As he got closer, he stopped and motioned for Lisette to sit down.

"John will take you to the pre-op room. If there's anything else I need, I can probably get the information from your husband." She nodded toward David.

Lisette wanted to correct her, but the wheelchair was already in motion.

When Lisette was dressed in a crisp, white hospital gown, she gulped and figured that she was as ready as she could be for the blessed event. The sterile, antiseptic smell of the pre-op room almost made Lisette nauseous or maybe it was her nerves doing that. Lisette didn't know which one. Curtains were draped around her gurney bed so she couldn't see any other patients, but she could hear other patients not too far away. She heard a lady's voice asking for pain relief, but Lisette didn't know for what. A few moments later, the anesthesiologist came by and began the process of the epidural. Lisette wished that she could have general anesthesia, but Dr. Berger had already explained to her that an epidural was best. Then two nurses came in to begin all the other preparation procedures.

One nurse looked at Lisette and spoke. "I saw you when you came in. Did your husband have to leave? Because if he's here, he can be in the operating room with you."

Lisette's face flushed. "Oh...he's not my husband...he's just a friend."

The nurse's expression seemed like she didn't know what to say to that. All she said was, "Oh."

Lisette was glad because she didn't want to talk about the details.

Another few minutes ticked by and Lisette was wheeled toward the operating room. Her lower body had become numb. She took slow deep breaths as they were pushing her. Lisette had never liked hospitals very much. As soon as they reached the operating room, she was shown a mirror that was angled in such a way she could see the baby when it showed up. Lisette nodded that she understood but then closed her eyes tight. She didn't want to see anything while she was in there, including the baby. Intense nervousness was enveloping Lisette.

Lisette kept her eyes closed and felt nothing during the entire Caesarean. She may have even dozed off. When her eyes opened again, she heard the rolling wheels against the tile floor. Then she noticed that she was in the recovery room and a nurse was attaching an I.V. to her left arm. Then another nurse came over and asked if Lisette would like to see the baby.

"Umm...can I wait until I'm in my regular room?" Lisette wasn't ready to see the baby yet.

The nurse squinted at her and pulled her head back about an inch or two. Lisette guessed that she was confused because most women wanted to see their babies right away. Lisette wasn't most women. Her situation was very different. She felt the need to explain, so she added, "It's just that I feel a little weak and I want some strength back first."

The nurse nodded and walked away as if Lisette's answer satisfied her.

Lisette wished she could stay here in this bed forever—with no worries or stresses. She dozed off again.

When she woke up, she was in a regular hospital room. Dr. Berger had already prepared her she would have to stay in the hospital for about four days afterward. Lisette wondered if maybe a week might be more in order because as the anesthetic was wearing off, she was feeling a good deal of pain.

As if on cue, Dr. Berger walked into the room. "How are we feeling?"

"It...it's hurting, Doctor."

Dr. Berger walked around to the left side of the bed and reached for a button controller. He laid it near Lisette's hand. "Push this button whenever you feel pain. It will release pain medication through your I.V."

Lisette nodded and reached for the button to press it immediately. Relief came. She closed her eyes again.

Lisette awakened to the sound of another nurse standing over her, holding a baby in her arms. She was almost singing. "I bet you've been waiting to meet this little one."

Lisette nodded because that was what was expected of her.

The nurse maneuvered the bed controls to raise Lisette up while holding the baby within her arms. She laid the baby onto Lisette's lap in such a way it wouldn't press on her incision. Then she announced, "It's a girl. You have a beautiful daughter," in the same sing-song cadence as before.

"A girl?" Lisette said as she stared down into the face of a little baby. My daughter? The baby was swaddled in a bright, clean white gown with a little pink hat hugging her tiny head. A few warm tears automatically flowed down Lisette's cheeks, but those tears weren't her familiar ones of sadness. Those tears were different somehow. But then Lisette noticed something. This baby wasn't even a day old yet and Lisette could already see Roger's square jaw on her tiny little face. Lisette's tears morphed back into the soft sobs of sadness she was used to. Her mouth whispered, "Roger, Roger, Roger."

The nurse reacted to the distress by sweeping the baby out of Lisette's arms. "I'll be right back, miss." She swiftly exited the hospital room with the baby in her arms but came back in almost as quickly. Lisette was still silently weeping even though her vocal cries had diminished.

"Are you okay, Ma'am?" The young nurse was visibly shaken by the unusual reaction.

Lisette sniffed to stifle more cries.

"Umm...I'll go get someone," the nurse offered.

Dr. Berger walked in a few moments later and picked up Lisette's right wrist to feel its pulse. He said it was a little slow but nothing to be alarmed about.

Lisette didn't react to that news.

"Lisette Carter, can you hear me?" Dr. Berger persisted.

Lisette finally nodded.

"Are you feeling weak from the procedure? Does anything hurt?"

Lisette shook her head.

"Well, do you feel okay?"

"I...I'm frightened," Lisette whimpered.

The doctor picked up her hand and caressed it. "It's normal to be scared and nervous. You're a new mommy."

"It...It's normal?"

"Of course." He continued to rub her hand gently in a circular motion.

Lisette sniffed. The tears were drying up.

"Now, don't you want to see that beautiful little girl of yours?" he coaxed.

Lisette was still scared and sad that Roger wasn't there to see their little girl, but she wanted to see the baby. She forced the corners of her mouth up as she nodded her head like an obedient soldier. She had to be brave. And she shouldn't be scaring young nurses with her adverse, unusual reactions. She forced herself to breathe in and out deeply.

Dr. Berger patted Lisette's hand one last time, smiled, and turned to head out of the room.

CHAPTER 15

The same young nurse came in again holding Lisette's baby but looking nervous because she didn't know what her patient's reaction this time would be. However, Lisette reached out and tried to cradle the little thing in her arms. When she looked down, she still saw that square jaw of Roger's. Lisette bit the edge of her tongue to keep from crying again.

She stared down at the little pink hat, the little forehead, closed eyes, a tiny button nose, and puffy little cheeks that had a blush of pink on them. The baby's lips were pursed. She was beautiful. Lisette smiled. Visible relief showed on the young nurse's face. This was more of the reaction she was used to seeing.

The nurse left the room. Lisette looked down again and her eyes soon became glued to that little face. She touched the corner of the baby's mouth and the lips twitched. She stroked one eyelid which made both eyelids flutter.

The baby's eyes opened, and she made a gurgling sound. A tiny squeak of delight popped out of her mouth. Lisette closed her eyes as a wonderful peace washed over her. She couldn't describe it, but it felt good. When Lisette opened her eyes again, the baby's eyes were still open, and she seemed to watch Lisette. Lisette held her gaze and felt more warmth flowing through her body.

"I guess I need to think up your name." Lisette cooed. Another thing to worry about. What if she picked the wrong name? Roger would have known how to pick out a good name. Lisette sighed.

But Roger wasn't here, and this baby girl still needed to be named. Lisette focused on her tiny face. "What do you want to be called?" She cooed again knowing full well that the baby didn't know what she was saying. The baby smiled again though.

The young nurse returned and asked, "Would you like to breastfeed?"

Lisette spoke, "Yeah, I guess, but I don't know what I'm doing."

"There's nothing to worry about. If it works and you like it that's great. And if it doesn't work, and sometimes it doesn't, that's okay too. Don't put any pressure on yourself. Just try to relax."

Lisette nodded, and the nurse helped to position her on her side with the baby next to her. The nurse helped Lisette open and loosen one side of her gown. Even though she was young, the nurse seemed adept at helping new mothers. As soon as the baby was placed close enough, she suckled immediately. The nurse smiled, and Lisette's eyes widened as she cradled the baby's head. The nurse positioned the gown a little better to make the exposure as little as possible. Lisette marveled at the fact that she was feeding her baby and it seemed effortless. Maybe this was a sign that some things did come naturally.

Later, Lisette was alone again in her hospital room. She took out her fuchsia journal and pen.

I saw you for the first time today, little girl. You are so beautiful even your little square jaw. That jaw will always remind me of your wonderful father. I'm glad you have it. I hope Roger is looking down on you right now and smiling at the wonderful creature we created together.

Sandra sprung into the hospital room carrying a big pink package with a white bow. "Hi, it's Auntie Sandra," she exclaimed.

Lisette smiled at her friend. "Hi, thanks for coming, Sandra."

Sandra's eyes dropped to spy the suckling infant in Lisette's arms. "Well, well, I guess she's a little busy to say hi." Sandra giggled and set the wrapped package down on the side table.

Lisette continued to smile and look down at the baby.

Sandra crossed her arms in front of her. "Well look at you, I knew you'd be a natural at this mommy thing."

Lisette sighed. "I don't know about that. I'm so nervous and I don't even have a name for her yet." She paused. "Doesn't a mother usually pick out a name before they even get to the hospital?"

Sandra made a playful tsk sound. "Oh, you'll think of one. Just relax. Something will come to you."

The baby stopped sucking. "Don't you want any more?" Lisette spoke as she positioned her back at her breast. The baby didn't take it this time. Lisette's face tensed.

"She's probably just full," the young nurse assured Lisette as she helped her to reposition the baby and close her gown. "She'll probably fall asleep in your arms now. Do you want that, miss?"

Lisette nodded, and the nurse left the room.

Sandra filled her in on what she had missed at the diner. Not much. The diner always seemed to hum along like clockwork no matter what. "And speaking of regular customers, one of them has been in the hospital waiting room for a long time." Sandra gave a sly smile with a knowing look.

Lisette's nose crinkled up. "Huh? Is David still here?"

"Still?"

"Well, he drove me here this morning, but I figured that he left a long time ago."

Sandra rolled her eyes. "You think he'd leave?"

"Well, yeah. He's got things to do."

"I don't think any of those things are as important as you." Sandra smiled again. "I asked him if he wanted to come in and see you before I did. He told me no. He'd wait. And that I should enjoy my time with you first. He's a very nice man, Lisette."

Lisette's nose crinkled at Sandra's meddling.

"Lisette, the man likes you. Just give in to it. He's a really great guy."

Lisette looked down and saw the square jaw again. "It's not that simple."

Sandra puffed out her cheeks and released air.

"I know, Sandra, you don't think it's a big deal, but it is a big deal." Lisette lifted the baby up about an inch for emphasis. "This is a big deal. And this is Roger's. He wouldn't want his baby with someone other than him."

"Lisette." Sandra calmed her breathing and tone as best she could. "Roger would want you to be happy."

At the word happy, Lisette's mind jumped to one morning about a year ago when Roger was leaving for work. Lisette had walked closer to him to wish him a good day. Roger had kissed Lisette's lips and then told her, "You have a happy day too, sweetie."

Lisette shook her head back to reality and Sandra's seemingly smug face as she admitted an ounce of defeat. "Maybe."

"Well, that's better than nothing. Happiness is a decision made one day at a time. You'll get there, honey." Sandra leaned down, kissed Lisette's forehead and gently rubbed the baby's head. "Now, I'll get out of here so *other* people can visit with you two, but I will be back tomorrow." Then she added, "If Bob is okay with me being away from the diner again."

"Bye, Sandra. Thanks again for coming."

◆ ◆ ◆

David entered Lisette's hospital room a few minutes after Sandra left. Lisette wondered if Sandra said anything to him as she was leaving. She knew Sandra cared for her but was it right she kept on pushing David and her together?

What would Roger think? Lisette heard Sandra's voice answer that question. *Roger would want you to be happy.* Lisette shook her head.

"Hi, Lisette, I saw Sandra leave. Are you still okay with having visitors?" David asked.

Lisette nodded.

"Good. Cause I want to see that little baby." David walked closer.

Lisette looked down to make sure that her gown was still covering everything. It was.

David reached out and touched the pink hat and then touched the baby's cheek. "She's so soft."

Lisette smiled a proud smile. "Yeah, isn't she pretty?"

David nodded. "She takes after her mama."

"I don't know about that." Lisette brushed away the compliment as swiftly as she could.

David kept staring down at the baby. "I definitely see your button nose, Lisette." As David spoke, he touched the tip of the baby's nose and then also mine.

The touch of David's warm finger gave Lisette a tingle. If David would be around Lisette a lot, she could save money on make-up because she wouldn't need to buy anymore blush.

The young nurse returned just then. "You've been up for a while now, miss. The doctor would like you to take regular naps. Remember, you are recovering."

"Okay, I am a little tired and my incision is aching." Lisette was also secretly grateful for the nurse's interruption because it meant that David would have to leave, without her having to ask him to.

The nurse lifted the baby and pointed toward the I.V. bag with her head. "You can use your pain reliever button any time."

Lisette reached over to get it as the nurse disappeared with her baby.

"That's my cue. I'll be going too," David obliged. "Can I visit you again tomorrow?"

"Of course, you can, David, but you don't have to," Lisette said.

"No, I want to."

Suddenly Lisette remembered what David had said earlier that day. "David, is today really your birthday?"

David smiled. "Yes, and it's been a wonderful day."

That really is an amazing coincidence, Lisette thought to herself but all she said was, "Happy birthday."

"Thank you."

"Oh, one more thing, David. Didn't you have to work today?"

"I took a vacation day."

"Huh?"

"I wanted to help you if you need it."

"Why?" Lisette questioned him.

David looked down toward the white tile flooring. His gaze stayed there as he spoke. "This is cathartic for me, Lisette. The last time I took a lady to the hospital to have a baby, it didn't turn out so good. But now I have a better memory of a hospital." Then his gaze lifted. "But if I get to be a burden, I'll back off."

Lisette interrupted him without thinking. "You're not a burden, David." His being there for her meant more now since Lisette knew he was facing his own demons.

David smiled at that and then added, "Thank you. Oh, and Lisette?"

"Yeah."

"I can also give you and the baby a ride home when you're released. Don't say no. I got you here and it's my responsibility to get you back home," David dutifully reported.

"Okay." Lisette didn't want to admit it, but it did feel good to be taken care of again.

Lisette's thoughts drifted to Roger. Roger had always said it was his responsibility to take care of her. What would he think of another gentleman offering his services to do that?

CHAPTER 16

Lisette tossed and turned. She wanted to blame it on pain from her incision, but her pain relief button was working. However, it wasn't working on her interior pain. She stared at the ceiling tiles. She tried counting them to make herself sleepy but all that accomplished was knowing that there were 210 tiles. She didn't know what she would do about the baby, or about David.

After finally getting a few hours of sleep, she awakened to an older, gray-haired nurse bringing a beautiful bouquet of a dozen pink roses into her hospital room.

"What are those for?" she asked.

"I just bring them in. I don't send them. But there's a card." The older lady smiled dutifully and handed the card to Lisette.

Lisette held out her right hand for her to drop the card in. "Thank you." Lisette waited for the nurse to leave the room before she took a whiff of one of the beautiful pink roses. She had always loved roses, especially pink ones. The sweet smell enveloped her nose.

Before Lisette had a chance to read the card, the gray-haired nurse came back into the room and walked to the other side of the bed to check the I.V. bag. Then she said, "The doctor said the I.V. can come out today but you can only have a liquid diet." She took the tubing out of Lisette's arm and pulled the I.V. rack out of the room.

Lisette stretched out her left arm. It had been in the same position for most of the night. She started to pick up the flower card when she noticed blood gushing from her left wrist where the nurse had just removed the I.V. In a panic, she pressed the call button.

The gray-haired nurse returned.

Lisette pointed to her arm.

The nurse moved quickly and in no time at all Lisette's wrist was clear of blood and wrapped.

Finally, Lisette focused on the little card. It read, *Pink roses for a beautiful mom and her new baby. David.* Warmth crept up Lisette's neck onto her face. Why did this man have to be so sweet?

Just then Lisette heard a familiar voice saying, "Hello" from around the corner. She couldn't place it at first. It was much throatier than Sandra's voice. Seconds later, her mother-in-law, Sylvia Carter, rounded the corner and announced, "Oh Lisette, I wish I could've been here sooner." She then shrugged her rounded shoulders. "But I'm here now and I'm here to help."

"Uh...thank you for coming, Sylvia. It's been awhile." Lisette wondered what she meant by help but was afraid to ask. When Lisette had lived in her basement, Sylvia was always trying to help her with something. Help may not have been the best term. What she did was try to take over.

"Yes, I know, dear, I wish I could've talked to you more throughout this pregnancy. I know at the beginning of it, I told you I could help. I haven't been feeling so well...you know...distress over my Roger. But when I remembered your due month, I kept on calling the hospital to see if you'd arrived yet and finally you did. I wanted to see my grandbaby. That might cure a lot of what ails me."

She spoke the words grand baby with a touch of giddiness uncharacteristic of her. But everything else she said came out sounding sad. Sylvia had always been a little on the aloof side. Her lips were thick and seem to pinch up when she tried to smile. Pity for Sylvia shot through Lisette.

Lisette politely smiled back and tried to console her mother-in-law. "That's okay. You're here now, when it's important."

"Well, where is the baby?" Anxiousness stirred Sylvia's face.

"I can call the nurse and ask if she can bring her in." Lisette reached for the nurse call button and pressed it.

Sylvia straightened her shoulders and did her best to shake off much of the sadness that Lisette had just seen. "So, how have you been, my dear?" Sylvia stood about two feet away from Lisette. Sylvia Carter had never been the touchy-feely type. Hugs never came easy for her. She was always more of a helpful and practical type.

"I'm good. A bit overwhelmed now but I guess I'll be okay as I get used to this mother thing." Lisette tried to hide some of her anxiety. She didn't want to worry Roger's mother.

"I'm sure you'll be okay. You were always a good girl." Sylvia's tone sounded condescending, but Lisette didn't think she meant it that way. Sylvia had always made a habit of calling her a girl, not a young lady or young woman, but girl, even after her and Roger had married.

The nurse saved Lisette from having to comment just then. Through the intercom, Lisette heard, "Did you need something, miss?"

Lisette smiled as if she could be seen through this speaker. "Yes, my mother-in-law would like to see the baby. Can you bring her in?"

"Yes."

Sylvia's face lit up. "Did I hear you say it's a girl?"

Lisette nodded.

"Oh," Sylvia began. "I'd always wanted to have a little sister for my Roger but alas it never happened."

At the word Roger, both Sylvia and Lisette looked down with somber expressions.

Lisette looked up first and tried to make a joke to lighten their moods. "Roger might not have wanted a little sister getting into his things anyway, Sylvia. Remember how possessive he could be with some of his things?" Lisette offered Sylvia her right hand, palm up and open, in a gesture of consolation.

Sylvia continued to look downward and didn't accept Lisette's hand. She didn't even pretend to smile. A sting of rejection coursed through Lisette.

After a couple of minutes, Sylvia shook her head as if she could knock old memories out. "Well anyway, we both have to move on."

Lisette had hoped that their individual griefs could be confirmed by a touch or a hug or something. They had both lost Roger, not just Sylvia.

The nurse interrupted again by walking in with the baby.

Sylvia intercepted the precious cargo in a swift and smooth manner. "Oh, there she is. Oh, can I hold her?" The baby was in her arms before an answer came.

The nurse looked at Lisette and silently seemed to ask if that was okay. Lisette nodded, and the nurse backed up to exit the room. Sylvia was already cooing a long string of nonsensical baby talk as if no one else was in the room.

Lisette delighted in a grandmother snuggling with her grandchild. Sylvia didn't typically look happy. The main way to describe her would be content but proper. To see her bubbly was a welcome change.

Sylvia went on cooing and giggling as she wandered to the chair against the wall across from Lisette's bed. A twinge of loneliness came over Lisette's heart as she watched her baby being cuddled by someone else.

Lisette shook her head with the realization she still didn't have a name yet. She decided to use Sylvia's abandonment as a quiet moment to think. She should, at least, come up with a name before she left the hospital. With a deadline, maybe she would think harder. She had always liked the name Mary, so simple yet pretty. Her best friend in elementary school was named Stephanie. She had always liked that name too. But throughout her pregnancy she kept thinking of a name that began with an R in honor of Roger. If it had been a boy, she would have named it Roger. That would have been easy. Roger's sweet face came into her mind once more and he was smiling. Maybe that was a sign that an R name would be best. She didn't know which R name though. There's not an exact feminine version of the name Roger.

Lisette looked up from her thoughts and Sylvia was still cuddling with the baby. If Lisette had her druthers, she would have wanted to hold the baby now herself, but she didn't know how to say that, so she waited.

As if Sandra knew Lisette needed moral support, she walked into the room and occupied Lisette's mind by leaning down and hugging her friend's shoulders. Lisette hugged back. Sylvia didn't even seem to look up at the new visitor. She was too preoccupied gushing over her grandchild to notice anyone new in the room.

"Well, girl, how does it feel to be a mommy for the second day?"

The word girl didn't bother Lisette when Sandra said it. There wasn't an ounce of pretension in

Sandra's voice, only pure camaraderie. "It feels good, I guess. They took away my pain medicine though."

Sandra looked concerned. "Does it still hurt?"

"No, not right now. But I'm afraid it'll come back again."

"Good, I'll be praying it doesn't." Then Sandra nodded toward Sylvia and the baby and squinted her eyes as if to ask who that was.

"My mother-in-law stopped by to see her granddaughter," Lisette explained.

Sylvia looked toward the two of them and gave what Lisette would call a strange look.

Lisette continued, "Sandra, this is Sylvia. Sylvia, Sandra."

Sylvia looked up again, smiled with closed lips, and nodded before going back to playing with the baby. Lisette supposed a first grandchild could be enveloping.

Sandra said, "Hi ya," in her typical friendly demeanor even though Lisette could tell that she was a little miffed at being ignored. If Sandra had one downfall, it was that she hated being ignored. But she was able to control herself and turned back to Lisette. "So, have you decided on a name?"

"I was just trying to think of one. No luck yet."

At that, Sylvia looked up again. Even though she was not paying attention to Sandra and Lisette, Lisette felt she was listening to every word. "Oh, you should name her Margaret. Roger always loved his Aunt Margaret."

The only time Lisette had heard Roger speak of

his Aunt Margaret was when they were filling out wedding announcements. He had said she was nice, but he had never gushed over her. He hadn't even recounted any childhood stories about her. Lisette had no reason to believe Roger would have wanted that name for his child. Lisette said, "Hmm, that's a thought," to pretend she was considering it though. Then Lisette continued. "But I was thinking of an R name to honor Roger though."

"I think that would be just dandy," Sandra affirmed.

"But I don't know which R name." If naming her was hard for Lisette, how in the world was she going to raise her. Lisette sighed.

"Well, you will. No pressure. Just name her before she goes to school, so she'll know when they call the roll." Sandra kidded with Lisette. Her joviality eased some pressure.

She snickered. "I would hope I can name her before then. But with the trouble I'm having I'm not so sure." As Lisette spoke, she could see Sylvia out of the corner of her eye. She didn't look amused at their jokes. Lisette added, "Honestly, there aren't many ideas on the blank slate inside my head, maybe it'll be a long time before I think of one." She tried to laugh again to convince people she was still kidding.

"You'll think of one sooner than you think. I'll pray that a great name just comes to you." Sandra assured. "Well, Lisette, I wish I could stay all afternoon, but I'd better get back to the diner. Bob's ex-wife is filling in for me and, you know her, she can only wait tables for a short time before she loses it," Sandra quipped.

"What's the deal with them?" Lisette wondered aloud. "They've been divorced for a few years now. Why is she still around? Wasn't it her that left him?"

Sandra leaned closer to Lisette and whispered. "I think he feels sorry for her if you can imagine that. She leaves him for another man, asks him for a divorce, gets it, and then still asks Bob for favors. He is just too nice for his own good." Sandra rolled her eyeballs upward.

"Maybe he wants to get back with her?"

"I don't think so, Lisette, he seems to pity her more than anything else. But just between you and me, I think she takes advantage of his niceness." Sandra rolled her big brown eyes again for even more emphasis. But then her face visibly softened.

Sandra felt guilty if she was in any way mean to another person even when that other person got on her last nerve. "But at least she does fill in at the diner at times to help him out. Maybe she feels guilty sometimes or something."

Lisette had seen Bob stealing glances of Sandra many times in the diner and she had also seen the reverse even though Sandra hadn't admitted any feelings for Bob. Lisette had always pictured Bob and Sandra making a great couple. Regardless of that though, Lisette hoped Bob's ex-wife didn't hurt him again. He really was a nice man.

As Sandra got ready to go, Lisette said, "She should just leave him alone. Thanks for coming to see me again, Sandra."

"I'm hoping to come again tomorrow, girl, but if I

can't get here, I'll call you." Sandra lifted her right fist toward her ear as she spoke the word call and then she also spoke over her shoulder as she sauntered out of the room. "Bye, Lisette."

◆ ◆ ◆

After Sandra left Lisette's hospital room, Sylvia got up and walked toward the bed. She positioned the baby so that Lisette could take hold of her. Lisette took hold of her before Sylvia changed her mind.

"Lisette, I'd better be going as well but when do they discharge you?"

"I think on Thursday afternoon."

"Okay then, I'll be back then to drive you home." Sylvia informed her as she turned to go.

Lisette remembered David's promise and called after her. "But Sylvia..."

Sylvia turned back around to face Lisette. "What?"

"Someone is already driving me and the baby home."

Sylvia squinted. "Oh," Sylvia began as she tried to compose herself. "Then I'll just come to your apartment on Thursday evening."

"Apartment? Thursday evening? Huh?"

"Why, of course, I'll stay with you for at least a month."

Lisette's jaw dropped open.

"You will need help." Sylvia spoke matter-of-factly and turned again to head out of the hospital room.

Lisette knew that statement was true, but she'd

never considered the possibility of Sylvia helping her. She hadn't heard from her in months until now. But then she was the baby's grandmother and Lisette's own mother wasn't nearby.

After the nurse came back and got the baby, Lisette reached over and got her fuchsia journal and pen.

Your grandmother, your dad's mother, came to visit you today. She is a nice woman although she is very distant and standoffish sometimes. But she surely raised a great son and she let me live in her house, in their basement apartment, during my college years.

Your other grandmother, my mother, left for California right after I graduated high school. She had originally wanted me to go with her when she started her new life, but I couldn't bear to leave your dad. My dad left her when I was barely a teenager. She did her best to raise me after that, but she never felt complete without a man in her life so off to California she went to pursue one. She sends me postcards and letters a few times a year, but I don't think she's found anybody yet. Maybe if she'd stop running everywhere, someone would find her?

Sometimes I worry about this dysfunctional world you've been born into. Things don't happen as they should.

Baby, I worry for you because you won't have a daddy either. At least I had my daddy in my early years. I wish you could have known your daddy. He was so wonderful. He would have been good to you and for you. I hate that you'll grow up without your dad.

A tear slipped down Lisette's cheek as she closed the journal. How was she going to do this all by herself?

CHAPTER 17

Lisette dressed in a pair of dark blue shorts and a white tee shirt she hadn't had on since last summer. The shorts had been big last summer but now, with the extra weight, they fit fine. It felt good to be in non-maternity clothes and out of a hospital gown. Her doctor gave the okay to leave and David was coming at two o'clock to pick Lisette and the baby up. Lisette had wanted to name the baby before she left the hospital, but she still didn't have a clue. However, she knew it had to be an "R" name.

It was the first day she was allowed solid food. The orderly had brought her chicken noodle soup and a ham and cheese sandwich. It was bland, but it tasted good to Lisette. While she was eating, Lisette looked at her wilted pink roses and thought of the name Rose. That was a very nice name but didn't feel right. The name Rachel also came to her mind because she had always liked that name but that didn't seem right either.

Suddenly Lisette's favorite childhood book, *Re-*

becca of Sunnybrook Farm, came to mind. Just remembering the title brought a smile to Lisette's face. *Rebecca of Sunnybrook Farm* had been her favorite book as a girl. Rebecca was fun and joyful and brought smiles to people. That would be perfect for her baby daughter. She'd already brought smiles to everyone who had seen her. Rebecca. She would be Rebecca. Rebecca Carter.

Lisette willed herself to remember to call her mom out in California when she got home to ask her if she still had a copy of that book. She had said it had been her favorite book as a child too. Lisette knew it was a long shot since her mom's new life didn't have room for such childish books. Maybe Barnes and Noble had one. No matter what, she would get a copy for her little Rebecca.

David came in and Lisette smiled at his typical punctuality. She was glad he was her friend. The nurse brought Rebecca into the room, laid the sleeping baby on Lisette's lap, and said, "Bye bye, sweetie." Then she looked up at Lisette. "And good luck to you with this beautiful baby."

"Thank you," Lisette replied.

"Looks like everyone is here. Are you ready to go home?" David asked.

"I think so but I'm nervous too. The nurses won't be at my beck and call at home."

"You said your mother-in-law is coming. I'm sure she'll be able to help with what you need."

Lisette sighed. "Yes, but that'll be different from the nurses." Lisette then reconsidered her hesitation and tried to look on the bright side. "But she wants to help, and she's always tried to be helpful in the past." Just not friendly, Lisette added to herself.

"You'll have lots of help, Lisette. Your mother-in-law, Sandra, and me." David smiled as he took hold of her suitcase, the pink diaper bag, and the little bag from the hospital with her pain pills in it. Lisette only had to carry Rebecca so when she stood up, she was ready to go. Lisette walked around the corner of her hospital room where a nurse was waiting with a wheelchair.

"Hospital policy," the nurse spoke.

Lisette sat down again.

She and the nurse waited in front of the hospital while David went to get his car out of the parking garage. He pulled up in his dark green Ford Fusion a few moments later and hopped out to help both of his passengers in. Lisette spied a gray baby car seat in the back seat with the infant attachment in place. "Where did you get a baby seat, David?"

"I bought it."

"Just to drive me home from the hospital?"

"Well no, I'm hoping to give you and Rebecca more rides." He flashed an innocent smile. Lisette's heart squeezed at David's thoughtfulness. But there was also a tug of guilt.

Despite her reservations, Lisette went along with it all. "You're pretty sure of yourself, aren't you?"

"Uh huh."

Lisette struggled with getting Rebecca into the infant seat. After a few minutes though, she figured out the steps and Rebecca was snug and secure. Then Lisette climbed into the front seat and buckled herself in.

As they got closer to her apartment building, David confided, "Lisette, this moment seems a little special. I finally get to take a lady and her baby home from the hospital. I didn't get to do that years ago."

"Oh David, I'm sorry if this brings up too many bitter memories for you."

"No, don't be sorry, Lisette. It's kind of healing for me." David glanced over at her and smiled.

Lisette returned his smile, "Then I'm glad I could be a part of this special moment."

When David pulled up in front of the apartment building, Lisette noticed Sylvia sitting on two large suitcases in front of the building. A feeling of dread came over her. "I guess I'd better go in. There she is."

Lisette turned her head in David's direction. "Thank you again for driving us home, David. It's nice not to have to call a cab."

"You're welcome. I wanted to help." David replied. "You'll be fine. I'm sure she'll be a great help to show you the ropes."

"Yes, she will." Lisette forced a smile.

"Oh, and Lisette?"

"Huh?"

"Umm...after you've had time to get settled in to your new routine, umm...would you want to go out with me again? That is if Sylvia is still here to watch Rebecca. And it can even be for a short lunch because I've heard new mothers are wary about leaving their baby early on." David's usual confidence morphed into the demeanor of a young high school boy.

Lisette glanced again at Sylvia's two large suitcases and figured that she'd still be here. She responded, "I'd like that, David, but I'm not sure. You're a great friend but I might need more time. Umm...to recover. I'm sorry." She looked down at her lap because she didn't want to meet David's eyes as she turned him down. A part of her wanted to say yes because David had helped her so much, but the other part still didn't feel right about it.

David breathed out with a sigh. "Take your time. I'm not going anywhere unless you want me to. I don't want to push you again."

"You're not, this time. Thank you for understanding, David." She didn't have the heart to tell him she would never be ready to date him, or any other guy for that matter.

Both got out of his car and David assumed the role of carrying everything but Rebecca into the building. Sylvia stood as they walked closer. Her pinched face looked irritated, but she said a polite, "Hi."

Lisette sighed again. The upcoming month would be a long one.

As soon as they all got up to the apartment, David said his goodbyes and turned to go.

"Good night." Lisette spoke. "And David, thanks again for all of your help."

David nodded and tipped an imaginary hat, a gesture that made Lisette smile. Then she remembered something. "Oh, David, I almost forgot to tell you. I thought of a name."

"What is it?" David leaned forward.

"Rebecca." The more Lisette said it, the more right it felt.

"That's a beautiful name. Very fitting. She'll be Rebecca of Sunnybrook Farm, except a city version."

"Thank you." Lisette couldn't believe he used her reference.

The elevator doors opened, and David smiled again before he stepped in.

When the elevator door closed, Sylvia walked over and took Rebecca right out of Lisette's arms. "Now, let me take a good look at this little one. Did I hear you say it's Rebecca?"

"Yes."

Sylvia nodded. Lisette couldn't tell if she liked it or hated it, but a sharp tug pulled on her heart. Why had she snatched Rebecca away from her like that? She could have at least asked first. Lisette wanted to say something, but Sylvia was already cooing to Rebecca and wouldn't have heard. Lisette's eyes rolled upward but she only said, "Maybe I should take a nap. I'm still a little weak."

"Hmm," Sylvia began as she looked in Lisette's direction. "Oh, yes, you go in your room and rest for a spell. You do look tired." Then she looked back down at the baby again. "We'll be all right, Rebecca, won't we? Yes, we will."

Lisette's eyes rolled back into her head again. She guessed the name was okay with her mother-in-law. Roger had always said his mother was protective. He had told Lisette that his mother had always tried to hold his hand often until he was almost twelve and couldn't stand it anymore. Lisette still remembered Roger's cheeks turning bright pink when he confided that to her. She smiled at the memory then she pondered that if Sylvia was that protective it may be a good thing she was here to help. And, Lisette knew nothing about raising a baby.

"Sylvia, I'm sorry that I don't have another bedroom, but the couch is a pull-out one. Will that be okay, or do you want to sleep in my bed and I'll sleep out here?"

Sylvia shook her head. "No, I'll be fine out here. You need your rest. But I think I'll slide the crib out here where I can get her in the middle of the night."

Sylvia's request sounded more like an order than a request. "Out here?"

"Why yes, I'll get up in the night with Rebecca, so you can get your rest, dear. You need to recover."

Lisette felt that tug in her heart again but relented. "Oh, okay."

"Good, now you go lie down for your nap and I'll go pull that crib into the living room."

Lisette walked into her bedroom. She felt like a child being sent to her room. But her incision was sore so lying down was a good idea. She would need her pain medication soon. "Umm, Sylvia, before you do that, can you get me my shoulder bag and bring it in? I need my pain meds."

Sylvia brought Lisette's bag into the bedroom and handed it to her. "Here you go."

Lisette reached in and pulled out the translucent orange bottle. Then she twisted the lid and poured out one pill.

"Oh, I'll go get you some water." Sylvia turned to go but came back in with a tall clear glass full of water.

"Thank you." Lisette swallowed the pill and then sipped the water. Then she laid down as Sylvia began to tug on the crib. The legs of the crib squeaked on the faux wood floor. Shortly, Sylvia and Rebecca's crib were out of Lisette's bedroom. So much for the perfect spot underneath Lisette's bedroom window.

CHAPTER 18

L isette was thankful for the door to her bedroom. As she closed it, a little relief from Sylvia's antics came. Lisette knew she meant well, and she also knew she would need her help, but the extra tension in the apartment was palpable.

She dug her cell phone out of her purse and then sat up leaning against the pillows on the bed. Then she found her mom's number and called her. Lisette knew she wouldn't be able to afford to come to visit but she felt like she needed to share this moment with her.

"Hello." Lisette's mom's voice sounded a little anxious.

"Mom? Hi. It's me, Lisette."

"Oh hi, dear, I'm just about ready to step out of the door. I've got a new date with a man that just might be the one."

Since the divorce, her mom had surmised that every man she'd dated was the one. At one time, she must have thought that about her dad too. "Oh...then...I won't keep you long, Mom. I wanted to tell you something quick."

"Anything, dear. Go ahead."

"Well...I had the baby. It's a girl." Lisette's voice sounded more nervous than excited.

"Oh, I didn't realize it was time already." Her mom paused. "Umm...I am sorry that I couldn't be there for you, Lisette. Can you email me some pictures?"

"Of course, Mom, I will. Umm..."

Her mom interrupted Lisette's next thought. "Oh dear, he's outside. Can I talk to you later, Lisette?"

"Yeah, Mom, sure."

"Okay then, wish me luck on this date," her mom spoke cheerfully like the two of them were college girlfriends.

"Yeah, good luck, Mom. I hope he's nice." Lisette spoke what her mom wanted to hear.

"Okay, bye. I'll talk to you later. Love you. Be sure to email those pictures."

"Love..." Lisette heard the call disconnect before she could continue. Lisette supposed some things were more important than the first time you become a grandmother.

Lisette didn't know why she was surprised by her mom's reaction. Ever since the divorce, she had been a different woman. She lived in a world that Lisette didn't know much about.

Lisette was thirteen when her parents called her into the living room and announced that they were getting a divorce. Announced was the right word. They matter-of-factly spoke about the end of their marriage.

After the announcement, Lisette sat on the green ottoman, looking down at her athletic sneakers. She had no questions or even any thoughts.

"Honey, are you okay with this?" Her mom's voice tried to soothe.

Lisette's eyes squinted as she looked at her like something just climbed out of her head. She wasn't okay with this. Her family would be no more.

Her mom tried to ignore Lisette's obvious glare. "Honey, everything will be okay. Me and you will go on living right here in this house at least until you finish high school."

"Oh...that's a relief." Lisette's sarcasm had been evident. She looked over at her dad then. His face was still and stern. "And...where will you be, Dad?"

"I won't be here. I think I'm going to Texas." He had spoken in the same way he would have said he was going to the convenient store for some milk.

"Texas? What's in Texas?" Lisette had bellowed.

"I need a new start. I can stay with my brother until I get a new job there."

Just like her mom, he also had a calm demeanor that infuriated Lisette. They were speaking calmly while her life was in ruins.

"You...You're never coming back?"

"I don't think so."

Lisette looked again at both overtly calm faces and wanted to scream.

"Honey, everything will be okay. We'll be just fine." Her mom continued in her attempt to soothe Lisette's confusion and pain.

Why weren't they hurting? They seemed like everything was fine. Didn't they realize that their family was breaking up? A hot tear had appeared in the corner of Lisette's eye.

"We'll be fine." Her mother repeated.

Was she trying to convince Lisette or herself? Lisette didn't know.

Dad stood up. "Well, I'll be leaving tomorrow. I have an early flight."

"Tomorrow, you're going tomorrow? Are you ever coming back for a visit?" Lisette pleaded.

Her dad's eyes caught hers for a moment until he turned his head away. He couldn't face his own daughter. "I don't think I'll be back, Lisette. But don't worry, I'll send your mom money each week to help care for you."

"Money! I don't want your money!" Lisette yelled. "What about being a family?"

Her mom placed a hand on her shoulder which Lisette flicked away.

"Honey, this isn't easy on any of us."

"It seems pretty darn easy on you two. You're both calm as can be!"

Lisette's mom continued, "It's not easy, dear, me and your dad just aren't meant to be together anymore. It's over."

"You're married! What about the 'till death do we part stuff? Huh?"

"Honey, we can't do it anymore."

Lisette looked over at her dad again. At least her mom was trying to comfort her. But her dad was just standing there. He even seemed to take a few steps backward to get away, like he couldn't get away from them soon enough.

"What about you, dad, don't you think a marriage means something?" Lisette yelled.

He shrugged his shoulders as he looked at the floor. No comment escaped his mouth until a few moments later, Lisette heard a murmured whisper come out of him. Maybe he hadn't meant to say it aloud, but he did. Lisette distinctly heard, "Marriage just isn't forever. Something will always mess it up."

Maybe it was just the innocence of childhood protecting Lisette's brain, but she still couldn't recall any clues that a divorce had been forthcoming until that day.

Her dad didn't say anything else. The next morning, he left the house with two suitcases and went to the airport. Lisette never saw him again.

CHAPTER 19

Lisette was just about asleep when her cell phone buzzed. Sandra's name flashed on the screen, so she answered it.

"Hey Lisette, I'm sorry I didn't get back to the hospital today. The diner got extra busy and I couldn't get away. Are you home now?"

"Yeah, I'm home." Lisette yawned. Her pain meds weren't going to allow her to talk for too long.

"Does the little one like her new home?" Sandra inquired.

"I don't really know. I'm in my bedroom and she is out in the living room with Sylvia." Lisette hoped that didn't sound funny. Not being with her baby when she brought her home for the first time.

Sandra seemed to understand. "Well, you probably need to rest more. Your body has been through a lot in the last few days."

Lisette nodded.

Sandra continued, "I really don't want to keep you from your rest, Lisette." Her voice trailed off like her sentence wasn't complete.

"But?" Lisette managed to ask after hearing Sandra's audible deep breath.

"I kind of wanted to tell you something too."

"Shoot." Lisette's curiosity outweighed her sleepiness.

"Well, yesterday when I got back to the diner, after the hospital, I thanked Bob's ex-wife for filling in for me."

Sandra paused.

Lisette didn't think she was done. "And?"

"But then she went back into the kitchen and stayed there talking with Bob until closing."

"What were they talking about?"

"I don't know, Lisette, I wish I did." Sandra paused again. "You don't think they're getting back together again?"

Sandra's voice sounded melodramatic. Did she like Bob? Why else would she care if he talked to his ex-wife? "I wouldn't think so, Sandra. There's been a lot of water under that bridge."

"I know but it's weird...ya know?"

"Yeah, it is weird. Was she in the diner again today?"

"No, but Bob was quiet."

"Bob's always gruff and quiet, Sandra."

"This was different. He seemed contemplative like maybe he was thinking about getting back with her."

"I really don't think that sounds very plausible, Sandra." Lisette tried to assure her.

"I hope you're right."

"Umm...Sandra, do you kind of like Bob or something?"

There was a long pause that ended with Sandra saying, "I don't know."

Lisette smiled because she knew Sandra and Bob would be great together. "I hope I'm right about Bob not getting back together with his ex-wife. You don't need that complication while you're deciding if you know or not."

"Thank you, Lisette. Good night."

"Good night, Sandra." Lisette added, "I don't know if this will make any difference in your decision, Sandra, but I think you and Bob would make a great couple."

It felt good for Lisette to be on the other end of the nudge.

The next two weeks dragged by. Lisette stayed in bed a lot of the time. Her abdomen was sore. It seemed like the pain medication at the hospital was much stronger than the pain medication they gave her to take home. Anything that either pushed or pulled on her incision made her terribly uncomfortable. She took a pain pill every four hours like clockwork and wondered if it would ever stop hurting.

Sylvia was a godsend in those first weeks. She did everything for Rebecca and brought meals in for Lisette. She also brought Rebecca into Lisette's room a few times a day. Lisette could feed Rebecca one time a day by breastfeeding but had to supplement the other feedings with formula. The doctor assured her that happened sometimes, and it wasn't her fault but Lisette still worried. Maybe it was a sign she wouldn't cut it as a mother.

Lisette pondered the thought of making an adoption plan for little Rebecca often. She still didn't know if she was ready for a baby.

The doctor also ordered Lisette to walk around the apartment a couple of times a day to keep her circulation moving and to drink plenty of water. She did what she was told. The sutures dissolved nicely, as they were supposed to, but some pain remained.

Lisette lamented that her newest bottle of painkillers had "No Refills" written on the label. The doctor had told her he couldn't write her another prescription. She would have to make do with over-the-counter pain relievers soon. There were about three potent painkillers left so she figured that she had about twelve hours of comfort remaining and then she'd be on her own. Lisette liked the way the strong pills took the edge off her emotions as well as the physical pain.

She continued to write things in her journal book each day. It had helped her to think things through a little. One day she wrote:

I'm still contemplating if I should make an adoption plan for you, Rebecca. I don't think I can do this, you're a beautiful baby, and you deserve great parents. Two of them. Not just little old me. You deserve so much more.

When the pain medication ran out, Lisette began taking ibuprofen every four hours. Maybe she could fool her body into thinking it was the more power-ful pills. However, it wasn't the same. The ibuprofen didn't do much for her emotional pain. However, she clung to them anyway.

The pain diminished as the incision kept heal-ing, but the emotional pain escalated. Lisette had read that postpartum depression only lasted the first week after giving birth and if she experienced it later, she should seek a physician's advice. She didn't do that.

Lisette knew she was not experiencing post-partum depression. She was still experiencing post-Roger depression. It had started before she even knew she was pregnant. Therefore, she suffered in silence with a pretend smile. She was getting good at doing that.

Sylvia brought Rebecca into Lisette's bedroom. This had been the custom even when it wasn't breast-feeding time and Rebecca was taking a bottle. Sylvia carried Rebecca and the warm bottle to Lisette, so she could feed her, except at night when Sylvia let her sleep.

Lisette took Rebecca into her arms willingly and then held the bottle for her. Rebecca sucked continu-ously. She looked down at her child, still not believ-ing it is her child. Even at a young age, Lisette saw Roger's calm demeanor on Rebecca's little face. Roger always seemed calm no matter what he was going through. Lisette had always admired that. She, on the other hand, had always been anxious over every little thing.

Sylvia remarked, "Oh, how peaceful she looks."

"Uh huh, just like Roger." At the word Roger, Lisette's throat caught.

"He was calm about most things, wasn't he?" Sylvia mused along with her daughter-in-law.

Lisette nodded.

Both stared at the baby for a long moment. Thoughts of Roger continued to dwell in Lisette's mind and she assumed in her mother-in-law's too.

When Rebecca finished eating, she asked if she could keep her with her for a while longer. It seemed funny to Lisette to ask for permission to spend time with her own daughter, but it also seemed the appropriate thing to do since Sylvia had been in charge since day one.

Sylvia blinked twice but then spoke. "Why, of course, dear. That'll give me some time to clean up the living room and kitchen." With that, she left the room.

Lisette cradled Rebecca as she rose from the bed, walked to the door, and pushed it closed with her hip. There wasn't a chair in the small bedroom, so she came back to the bed to sit down. A full tummy had already caused Rebecca to close her eyes in sleep.

Lisette whispered to her anyway. "What am I going to do with you? You really are a beautiful baby and you deserve better. You deserve a good daddy like Roger would have been. Oh Rebecca, you'll never know your daddy. And if I give you away soon, you won't remember me either. You'd be better off that way though. Some nice couple will see you and want you right away just the way I did when I first saw you."

Rebecca twitched her tiny pink mouth but stayed asleep.

Lisette continued her soliloquy, "I love you, Rebecca. But I love you too much to take a chance on ruining your life. You deserve more." With that, she cradled Rebecca a little tighter to her chest as a tear dropped onto the belly of Rebecca's pink onesie.

CHAPTER 20

"Hello?" David's familiar voice comforted Lisette. She knew she had called the right person. David could help her.

"David?" she whispered, not wanting Sylvia to overhear anything.

"Lisette, are you okay? Your voice sounds funny. Is everything all right with Rebecca?" Much concern accompanied David's question. Then he repeated, "Are you okay?"

Before Lisette spoke, she smiled at David's obvious concern. Some woman would be lucky to have him as a husband one day.

"Lisette?" David questioned again with even greater concern in his voice.

"Yes, David, it's me. Can you come by sometime?" She took a deep breath. "I need to talk to you about...umm...something." She paused again. "But it can be whenever you're free."

"I called you a few times over the past few weeks, but Sylvia said you were resting and still weren't up to company. Did complications come up in your recovery? Are you feeling better now?"

Why hadn't Sylvia told her that David had called? "I didn't tell her to tell people that. Umm...I didn't even know you had called."

"Oh, so you're feeling better?"

Lisette heard a tangible relief in David's voice.

"I am physically, I guess, but..." Lisette's voice trailed off. Maybe she shouldn't be talking to David about this. She could get on Roger's laptop and search for the information she needed to know.

"What? Lisette, are you okay?" David's voice raised with concern again.

Lisette wondered if David wanted off this roller coaster ride he was on with her. She nodded, forgetting she was on the telephone.

"Lisette? Are you still there?"

"Umm, yes," she finally spoke. "Can you come by sometime? Soon, if you can." She might as well just ask him for help.

"Of course, I can. It sounds important. I'll come by right after work this evening."

"Thank you, David," she said as she ended the call without saying bye. She was glad he didn't make her wait for days. The sooner she got answers about this, the better.

A few hours later, the intercom buzzer rang. Sylvia beat Lisette to it. Lisette heard her say, "Yes?"

"Uh...it's David. Lisette is...umm...expecting me."

"I think she's sleeping. Can you come back later?"

David spoke again, "She called me and asked me to come by. She said she had something important to talk about. Could you check to make sure she's sleeping, please?"

"Hold on, I'll go check," Sylvia's dry voice spoke.

Sylvia turned and gasped when she saw that Lisette was only a few feet from her. She turned back around without a word and pressed the intercom button again. "Umm...yes...she's expecting you." Then Sylvia turned back to Lisette. "What do I do now to let him in?"

Lisette stepped forward and pressed the white button to release the outer door downstairs.

In a few more minutes, David knocked on the apartment door. Lisette opened it and saw David standing there holding a cardboard tray with two white coffee cups from Cuppa Joe's. Last year, Lisette had gone to Cuppa Joe's a lot. She used to love their coffee. Then when she was pregnant, she stopped that habit just in case too much caffeine wasn't good for the baby.

David noticed her gaze at the two coffee cups. "I was in the mood for a coffee and didn't want to arrive with just one for me, so I got you a coffee au lait." Then David added, "But if you don't want or like it, you don't have to have it."

"Oh...thank you, David. That was very thoughtful. I used to go to Cuppa Joe's all the time before I got pregnant. This may just ignite my habit again." She picked up a cup out of the tray, smelled the aroma, and took a sip of the creamy goodness.

David smiled, feeling appreciated.

Then, Lisette got to her business with him. "David, thank you for coming. I need information and I think you can help me."

David seemed a little disappointed by Lisette's business-like demeanor. He swallowed before speaking, "What do you need, Lisette?"

Lisette looked over at her mother-in-law's judgmental stare. "It's a little private. Can you excuse us, Sylvia?"

Sylvia grimaced. "I have to be in here to watch the baby. But you can talk in the other room."

Lisette didn't understand Sylvia's attitude. This was her home and that was her baby. But Lisette didn't want to make waves, so she said, "Okay, we'll go in the other room to talk." As soon as those words came out of Lisette's mouth, she remembered that the only other room was the bedroom. Was it okay to bring a man in there? What would Sylvia think? And what would Roger think? Lisette considered taking David into the hallway to talk by the elevators.

David seemed to notice Lisette's hesitation. "Anything wrong?"

She took another sip of the coffee and shook her head to ease her own anxiety. "Nothing. Come on." She continued to lead David into the other room. She assured herself that she was just going to talk to him and it was a business matter, for crying out loud.

When they were both inside the small bedroom

with no chairs, David looked uneasy. Lisette closed the door. She had to. Sylvia would hear everything they said if she didn't and she couldn't take that chance.

David leaned against the wall and motioned for Lisette to sit on the bed. "You sit, Lisette. I'll stand. You're still recovering from surgery." David remained a respectable five to six feet away from Lisette.

Lisette was relieved by his consideration and didn't argue as she sat on the edge of the bed. "I won't keep you long, David. Didn't you say you were working towards specializing in adoption law?"

David's mouth opened as he stared at Lisette. "Lisette, why on earth would you want to know that?"

"I've thought about it and I've decided to make an adoption plan for Rebecca. It's the best thing." Lisette spoke quickly to get everything out. But then she paused and added, "I think."

"You think?" David questioned. "That doesn't sound like someone who has made up their mind."

"David, don't make fun of me. This is hard."

"Well, then don't do it." David's abrupt tone of indignation surprised Lisette.

"You won't help me? I thought I was your friend?"

"As your friend, I can't let you do that."

"David, I wasn't asking your permission. Why is it any of your business?" Lisette raised her voice a little but hoped it was still not loud enough for Sylvia to hear. Why would David even care if she gave up her baby? Wasn't that her decision? It definitely wasn't his decision.

David looked down at the wooden planks of the bedroom floor and was silent.

"David, I didn't mean to get so upset but why can't you help me?" Lisette pleaded.

"Lisette, I don't want you to do that. I think you'd regret it." David's voice changed from abrupt to soothing.

Lisette looked down and touched her left ring finger where her engagement and wedding rings used to be. After a few seconds, she admitted, "I just might."

"Well then, don't decide now, Lisette. If you give it more time and can convince me you are doing the right thing for you, then I will help you. But please make sure you're thinking clearly. It's a big decision and you're still recovering and everything."

Lisette's shoulders drooped two inches lower. "But I can't wait, David," she began with a shaky voice. "I can't wait."

David broke his unspoken promise to keep his distance and sat down next to her on the side of the bed. Their legs touched as David leaned toward her to comfort her. "Why can't you wait, Lisette? What's wrong?"

She buried her head in her hands as she leaned forward. "If I wait, I'll never do it." Lisette sniffled.

David rubbed her upper back to comfort her. He kept rubbing back and forth as if that was the only thing he knew to do. He wrapped his arms around her, in a cocoon like hug, while Lisette was still leaning forward. She continued to sniff while trying to get a hold of herself.

Finally, she lifted and turned her head to face David. His dark brown, caring eyes shown back at her.

David used the same hand that had been rubbing Lisette's back to wipe tears off her cheek. He forced the corners of his own mouth upward into a smile. "Everything will be okay, Lisette, No matter what."

"David, why are you always so nice?"

"I like you." He admitted as his smile broadened across his face.

"But you don't even know me."

David tilted his head to the right and shrugged both shoulders. "I know enough to know I want to get to know you better."

She sniffed again. "But David, I can't offer that."

"Why not?"

"Because...because..." her voice broke off into the empty air. She couldn't say she was married because...well...she wasn't anymore.

"See, you can't think of a reason why not," David said as he nudged her shoulder with his shoulder. "And I can't think of one either."

David was trying to make her laugh with his playful action but instead it made her cry more. She closed her eyes and sniffed again.

David gulped at Lisette's reaction. He tried to go back to rubbing her upper back for comfort but this time she stiffened at his touch. He stopped rubbing and brought his hand back to his own lap.

With a shaky voice, Lisette attempted to explain herself. "Don't you understand? I can't offer you anything. I can't."

David looked down at his lap. "Not even your friendship?"

"You want more than that, David."

David nodded. "Well, yes I do. But I'll take friendship if that's all you can give me."

"That's not fair to you."

"Let me decide what's fair to me, Lisette."

She continued, "David, you are a very nice man."

"But..." David interrupted, "You're not attracted to me. Is that it?"

Lisette shook her head abruptly. "No, that's not it at all. You're very handsome. I thought so when I first met you."

David's delight showed in a touch of red dotting each of his cheeks along with another smile.

"Don't smile like that, David. I still can't offer you anything."

"You keep saying that." David continued to smile.

"Well, I can't."

"You seem to be trying to tell me, so I'll just come out and ask. Why not?"

"Because...because I...because I have nothing to give." More hot tears streamed down her face. "It's all gone."

"Gone?"

"Yes, it's gone. That's also why I should give Rebecca up for adoption. It's gone."

"What's gone? Lisette, I'm sorry but I'm not understanding you."

"It's gone. Me. All of me is gone. There's nothing left to give. To you. To Rebecca. To anybody."

David sighed and lifted Lisette's chin with his hand. As he did, she turned to face him.

He wiped more of her hot tears away before he spoke. "You're not gone, Lisette. You're right here. Your beautiful face and eyes and golden hair. It's all here."

"But there's nothing inside. It's all gone. It's like the inside of me died with Roger." Sniffs and sobs continued. "All that's left is the part that does whatever it has to do to get by. That's all I have left. Robotic motion. There's not enough to give anybody else."

David turned Lisette more and wrapped his arms around her in a very warm hug, which Lisette couldn't resist. She allowed herself to rest her cheek on David's shoulder and wrapped her arms around his back.

They stayed like that for a long moment until Lisette pulled back.

David let her go as she pulled away, but his eyes locked onto hers. "Lisette, I'm going to make it my business to help you live again. I had to learn how to live again after Laura passed away, so I know a little of what you're feeling." David paused but then added, "Although I don't know everything because every situation is different. I'm not going to pretend that I know everything about your situation. But I know a little and maybe I can help."

Lisette didn't argue even though she doubted that what he was proposing was possible. She doubted that she'd ever feel anything but empty again. However, knowing David's story made her wonder if she might learn a little something from him. He seemed to have survived his own tragedy. "I hope you can, David."

"Just promise me you won't make any rash decisions about Rebecca right now."

"I won't."

Lisette walked David to the door of her apartment to let him out. "Thank you, David, you're a great friend."

David looked deep into her eyes. "You really are too, Lisette."

Lisette lifted the right corner of her mouth and shrugged her shoulders. What had she done for him? Had she ever been a good friend to him?

"I'll call you soon, Lisette." With that promise, David headed toward the elevator and Lisette closed the front door.

◆ ◆ ◆

Sylvia erupted. "Do you see a lot of that man?"

Her abruptness made Lisette jump. "Huh? What do you mean?"

Sylvia's eyes narrowed, and her body stiffened as she repeated her question, slower. "Do you see a lot of that man?"

Lisette's confusion made her squint her eyes at Sylvia. "What kind of question is that? I've only known him a few months."

"It seems longer. You're meeting him for a private rendezvous."

"What? Rendezvous? You don't know what you're talking about, Sylvia." Lisette tried to collect herself. She didn't want to yell at her mother-in-law, not after all the help she'd been.

Lisette attempted to speak calmly. "Sylvia, I appreciate your concern. I really do. But David is just being very nice. He's a friend."

Sylvia's face softened a little but still seemed distraught. "Well, be careful that he stays that way. Your husband hasn't been dead a year yet."

Sylvia's thinly veiled threat took Lisette by surprise. No one knows better than her how long Roger had been gone. How dare she? Lisette yearned to yell but restrained herself when she noticed Sylvia's grief-filled face.

Lisette's chin quivered as her initial anger turned into agreement. Her own sadness defeated her. "You're right, Sylvia," Lisette whimpered. Then she vowed to herself not to let David get too close. Even if they were just friends, she couldn't take any chances. She knew she had to make that vow for Roger's sake.

Lisette wanted to lie down. She looked over at Sylvia and asked, "Are you okay here with Rebecca for the night, Sylvia?"

"Of course," Sylvia straightened and sat up in perfect posture to compose herself.

Lisette nodded. "Do you mind if I lay down for a while then in my room?"

"Of course not. Go right ahead. I'll be fine."

You would think an apology for overreacting might have been given but Sylvia offered nothing. But maybe she was right. Lisette had no right to get involved with David not even as friends.

She walked into her room and shut the door. Then she sat cross-legged on the bed and reached for her journal book and pen.

Sylvia has settled the dilemma I'd been having. If Roger's mother doesn't think I should see David, I don't think I should either. I must need to linger with Roger's memory longer, maybe even forever.

At one time, I would have said Sylvia's contempt of David was a sign from God. I think it was a sign but not from God. I don't know if God gives us signs or not. He seems cold and distant. I realized that fact the day that Roger died.

There's no one like my Roger. Sweet and kind and helpful. David may seem to have those qualities but he's still not Roger. I think I'm supposed to date only Roger for life. He loved me, and I still love him. We were supposed to be together forever. I'm not allowed to think of another man like that again. Not even a nice guy like David. For Roger's sake. For Rebecca's sake. And maybe even for David's sake. I have nothing to offer him.

CHAPTER 21

Sylvia bought an infant carriage and had been taking Rebecca outside for some fresh air each day. One day, Lisette told Sylvia that she wanted to take Rebecca for her walk.

"You're not recovered yet." Sylvia eyed Lisette with concern. "You need to rest."

Lisette argued. "The doctor says I should walk more, and I think the fresh air will do me good too."

"Okay, I'll push her, and you can walk along with us." Sylvia looked like she was giving Lisette a great present.

"Sylvia, I want to take my daughter out for a walk by myself." Lisette insisted, not knowing how Sylvia might reply but not caring. It was her baby.

"You don't want me to go?" Self-pity exuded from Sylvia's question.

She was good at invoking Lisette's guilt but since Lisette knew she wasn't doing anything wrong, she stood her ground. "Well no, but don't be offended. I want to spend time with my daughter. Based on the last few weeks, she probably thinks you are her mom. You're always with her."

"I am just trying to help." Sylvia crossed her arms across her chest.

"I know. And I'm grateful. Thank you." Why did Lisette always feel as if she needed to apologize to Sylvia?

"Okay." Sylvia snapped as her shoulders slumped. "I'll just clean up some around here and make myself useful while you're out."

"You don't have to do that, Sylvia. You already do so much. Just sit and relax and read or watch TV or something. You deserve a break." Lisette smiled to lighten the heaviness in the air.

Sylvia shook her head. "No, I can't do that. There's too much to do and someone has to do it."

Not only was she making Lisette feel guilty for wanting to spend time with her own child but now she was trying to make her feel guilty about not helping around the house. Lisette didn't know what to say and it didn't matter anyway because Sylvia had already left for the kitchen.

Lisette picked up a sleepy Rebecca from her crib and placed her into the carriage where she tucked a yellow blanket all around her. Rebecca's lips pursed and then relaxed. Lisette wanted to believe her little baby was trying to blow her mommy a kiss. She smiled because she already loved this little child more than she could have imagined. She would have to begin spending more and more time with her, no matter what Sylvia thought.

She checked the pink puffy diaper bag to make sure it contained the supplies she might need on the walk. Diapers, wipes, changing pad, some folded plastic grocery store bags, some extra baby clothes, extra small blanket, tissues, anti-bacterial cleansing gel, two toys, and a baby bottle with water in it. So much for spontaneity. Lisette picked up the diaper bag and her purse and put both over her left shoulder. Then she pushed Rebecca out of the apartment for the first time.

Lisette stepped out into the crispness of a beautiful fall day. The sky was a deep blue without a single cloud. She decided to push Rebecca toward the diner to visit Sandra. Lisette wanted to see her friend. After Sylvia's curtness, Sandra's happy-go-lucky attitude would be like a much-needed medicine.

The sun was still warm for autumn, so Lisette stopped at Cuppa Joe's for an iced coffee. Cuppa Joe's is a very tiny store without any tables or places to sit down—just great coffee to go. Behind the counter was everything needed to make delicious coffee concoctions. She took her iced caramel mocha latte outside and sat down on the nearest available bench with Rebecca's carriage right beside her.

Lisette reached into her purse for an ibuprofen and took it with a sip of coffee. Her incision wasn't hurting badly anymore, but she wanted to prevent the possibility of it starting again. Plus, the act of taking medicine on a regular basis, seemed to calm Lisette's mind.

Rebecca opened her eyes full and bright as if she too wanted to experience this glorious day. Lisette obliged and lifted her out of the carriage and onto her lap. Rebecca's eyes remained wide as she seemed to study Lisette's face. Lisette melted with delight. If moments like these continued, she might lose her doubts about keeping Rebecca.

After a few loving moments, Lisette again bundled up Rebecca into her carriage and tucked the blanket all around her. "We'd better keep going. I'm sure Miss Sandra really wants to see you again and I know I want to see Miss Sandra."

When Lisette got close to the diner, she checked the baby's diaper to see if it was still clean. It was, so she pushed the carriage to the front of the diner, maneuvered the door open, and finally pushed the carriage inside.

Sandra looked up when she heard the rattle of the carriage wheels. "Girl, it's about time you brought that baby in here." Sandra ran over and hugged Lisette. Then she investigated the carriage and began cooing a hello to Rebecca.

When Lisette had seen mothers with carriages before she had always wondered if the mother felt neglected by all the attention that the baby received while they were almost ignored. Sandra was different though. She wouldn't ignore her friend. She always welcomed everybody.

Lisette settled into a corner table with Rebecca, so

they wouldn't be in the way of customers or Sandra's service. Sandra came over every opportunity she had to talk. Even Bob made an appearance out of the kitchen to congratulate Lisette.

"So, how are things going with your mother-in-law?" Sandra winked playfully.

"Well, she's really a great help, Sandra, I really can't complain. She's been doing almost everything for Rebecca." Lisette paused and then added, "She's great."

"But?" Sandra prodded.

Lisette breathed in deeply. "She really has been a great help with Rebecca, especially when I was too sore to do much but she's almost acting like it's her baby and I'm the helper." Lisette paused and sighed again. "Maybe I'm just being paranoid."

"I'm sure that's not the case. You're level headed, Lisette." Sandra reassured.

Lisette shrugged her shoulders. "Yeah, I guess so. I mean I practically had to beg her to get her permission to take Rebecca out for a walk today."

Sandra's eyes widened. "What? She's your daughter, Lisette. If she gets too pushy, you've got to put your foot down." Sandra smiled and then stomped her foot for emphasis before she turned to give a man his check.

Lisette checked Rebecca's diaper again. This time it was a little wet, so she put the diaper bag over her shoulder, picked up the baby, and headed for the ladies' bathroom. It was a one-person bathroom, but it had a Kid Kare baby changing station. She changed Rebecca relatively quickly even though she had trouble balancing the baby while reaching inside the diaper bag.

When Lisette returned to the table, the lunch rush was just about over. She knew Sandra would have a few uninterrupted minutes to talk. When the last lunch customer dropped his tip on his table and headed out the door, Sandra sat down across from Lisette in the booth.

"Now, where were we?" Sandra smiled. "Oh yeah, first I want to hold that precious little angel."

She looked at Lisette as if to ask for permission. It was refreshing. Sylvia never looked that way. Lisette smiled and nodded. "Of course."

Sandra cuddled Rebecca into her golden-brown arms.

"Oh, I wish I had a camera. That's precious." Lisette smiled with delight.

"Aunt Sandra can watch this one for you any time. There'll be plenty of opportunities to snap pictures like this." Then Sandra's attention diverted to Rebecca. "And I'm going to any time you let me."

"I'm sure I'll need to take you up on that sometime."

Lisette saw Rebecca's eyes close peacefully as she settled comfortably into Sandra's arms. Sandra started bouncing her ever so gently. Then she looked up and focused on me. "You were saying about the second mom at your place?"

"Yeah, she's just a bit too protective and controlling. I'd like to take over things with Rebecca, but I don't know if I can ask her."

Sandra let out a harrumph-like sound. "You don't

have to ask her. Just tell her, Lisette. It's your child."

"But it is her grandchild." Lisette felt some sympathy for Sylvia's cause. She's already sad over Roger. Lisette didn't want to make her any sadder.

"That's wonderful, but it's not the same thing. You are <u>the mommy</u>."

"I know...I know."

"There is an easier way, Lisette. Just begin taking over things--one thing at a time." Sandra looked down at Rebecca who had fallen asleep and added. "Actually, she probably expects you to do that."

"You're probably right, Sandra," Lisette hoped that she could go through with that plan without hurting Sylvia's feelings.

"Oh, I'm always right." Sandra laughed a loud infectious laugh.

Lisette laughed with her, which eased some of her pressure.

"Well, now we've got the mother-in-law problem out of the way, how about that cute David? Even though I don't think that refreshing drink of water is a problem."

Lisette gulped. The memory of David's warm, comforting hug flooded her brain. He was a problem to Lisette's peace of mind. He was very nice and cared for her and Rebecca but that could be the biggest problem of all. "I did talk to him the other day."

Sandra leaned two inches forward and smiled a knowing smile.

"Not like that," Lisette began, "I called him, so I could find out more about the possibility of adoption."

"What?" Sandra almost choked on nothing but her surprise.

"Don't worry, at least for now, he talked me into waiting to make that decision."

"Good, so he's cute and smart. Even more of a good thing."

Sandra was trying to get to the real topic at hand. She would like nothing better than to see Lisette and David go out again. Lisette could almost feel the hope exuding from her friend and blushed. "I told you, it's not like that."

"Uh huh," Sandra said with a nod of her head but disbelief in her tone.

"It's not." Lisette knew she sounded defensive and she wanted to change the subject. "But anyway, he is nice, that's all."

To Lisette's dismay, Sandra wouldn't let the subject drop. "Why are you so insistent that this isn't the man for you?"

Lisette looked down. No words came.

Sandra read her mind and responded with a sour look. "When are you going to realize that Roger would want you to be happy?"

When was Sandra going to stop saying that? "Not without him."

Sandra reiterated. "Roger would want you to be happy. It's you that doesn't want it."

"I just can't."

Sandra stood up, placed Rebecca into the carriage, and moved a chair next to Lisette. She placed a comforting hand on Lisette's shoulder. "You can, and you're even allowed, Lisette. You're allowed to live or else God would've taken you with Roger."

"But it's not fair." Lisette whined.

"I know. It's not." Sandra began simply. "It's not fair that Roger died. It's not fair you were left pregnant and alone. But...I believe...that God is in control even over tragedies and he can bring good things out of bad things."

"How can you be so sure?"

Sandra shrugged her shoulders. "Well, I can't be sure intellectually. But I can trust and have faith that a loving God is in charge and knows a lot more than I do."

"You mean that God planned for Roger to die and leave me alone?"

"No, I don't believe that, Lisette. I believe a messed-up world has all kinds of tragedies. God doesn't cause the tragedies but sometimes...he does allow them. But only because he can work good despite them."

"Hmm," is all that Lisette could say. In the past, she would have agreed with Sandra because she did believe in God, but her belief hissed out of her like a blown tire on the day of Roger's accident. Something about Sandra's belief softened Lisette's heart a little though. Sandra believed it so strongly and she had such peace.

"That's good advice, Sandra, thank you." She hoped that her admission would end this uncomfortable conversation.

Sandra just nodded and smiled. "It's not really my advice. I get it from my bible."

Lisette thought of her own bible. She had packed it away last November. It must still be in her closet though. Maybe she'd get it out when she got home.

"Well, I'd better clean up these tables so they're ready for the dinner group." Sandra changed the subject. She always called it the dinner group and the lunch crowd because lunch was always busier than dinner. "Plus, Bob might fire me for slacking off."

Lisette lowered her voice to almost a whisper. "Bob would never fire you, Sandra. You're too good at what you do. Plus, I think he might be a little sweet on you." Lisette winked and faked a jovial tone because she wanted to get the conversation onto Sandra and off herself.

"Bob?" Sandra sounded surprised, but her eyes grew wider and even sparkled. "You think?"

Lisette giggled. "It's just a hunch but yes, I think so."

"I don't think that's true." Sandra shook her head.

It was nice to see Sandra in the hot seat for a change.

Sandra continued, "But it is true that if I don't get this place cleaned up for dinner, I'll be in trouble."

Lisette stood to go but remembered something and stopped. "Sandra, what happened with Bob's ex-wife? Has she been in lately?"

"No, she hasn't been in." A sly smile took over Sandra's face.

"Oh good, then Bob will be free to ask you out."

"I don't know about that, Lisette."

Lisette smirked as she reached out to hug Sandra goodbye. Sandra hugged back with a strong squeeze. Then she added, "I can't wait until you're back here working with me again."

When Lisette left the diner, she walked through the harbor area. She noticed the two-story Barnes & Noble bookstore and remembered to check on a copy of <u>Rebecca of Sunnybrook Farm</u>.

Lisette purchased a nice hardbound, classic edition copy of the book for her daughter. Now she'd be able to read to her about her namesake, maybe multiple times. Hopefully, her little Rebecca would be imaginative and charming despite her not-so-perfect beginning, just like the Rebecca in the book.

Before she left the store, she got an iced caramel macchiato coffee for the walk home. Yum! Her habit was forming again. She could feel it. The coffee, as well as her resolve to take duties back from Sylvia, energized Lisette as she returned to her apartment.

CHAPTER 22

Sylvia wasn't in the apartment when Lisette got back. Lisette took advantage of the quiet moment and got Rebecca's crib back into her bedroom under the window where it belonged. That was a start in the right direction. She smiled at the thought of Rebecca waking to the morning sunlight.

When she went back to the living room, she found Rebecca still sleeping peacefully. She didn't want to wake her to put her in the crib, so she let her sleep in her carriage. She then sat down in the living room on the couch and reached for the remote. Then she scanned the channels for something to occupy time. She finally landed on a rerun of Full House.

Before the show was over, Sylvia's key clicked in the lock and the door opened. Lisette had given her Roger's old key. Sylvia walked in carrying bags of groceries and was noticeably startled when she saw Lisette. "I didn't know you'd be back home yet. How was your walk?"

Lisette muted the television before she spoke. "Oh,

it was a beautiful afternoon. I think Rebecca enjoyed the fresh air. We went to see Sandra at the restaurant."

"Hmm. That's nice." Sylvia didn't sound the least bit interested. "Well, I'd better put these things away." Then she disappeared into the kitchen.

Lisette shrugged and turned the volume back up as she looked toward Rebecca's still sleeping form and murmured under her breath. "We had a good time. Didn't we, sweetie?"

A few moments later, Sylvia emerged from the kitchen and interrupted the show again. "What do you want for supper, Lisette?"

She looked pleasant enough now, so Lisette smiled and said, "Anything. Whatever you want is fine."

"Okay, how about spaghetti?" Then Sylvia glanced into the carriage. "Why is the baby still in her carriage?" Then she looked around the room. "And where's her crib?" Her snippy tone returned.

"Oh, I put it in my room. I think she should sleep in there now." Lisette spoke nonchalantly as she gathered her courage. Then to change the subject she added, "And spaghetti sounds great. Thank you."

Sylvia's face seemed to contort in confusion. "She's been perfectly happy out here. Why would you want to change things so suddenly?"

Lisette took a deep breath of strength. "Sylvia, I want to sleep in the same room with my baby. That's all."

"But you need your rest, dear."

Lisette took note of Sylvia's placating tone. "I've rested enough." Conviction rose in her throat. She wasn't going to take no for an answer.

"Oh, I guess you don't need me anymore." Sylvia's voice turned into a dramatic whimper.

"Sylvia, I can still use your help. You've been great so far. I want to bond a little more with Rebecca, that's all." Lisette's resolve faded a little to make peace.

Sylvia puffed out air. "Okay, it's your baby. What do I know?" Then she turned to head back into the kitchen.

Lisette swallowed hard, not knowing what to say, so she went back to watching the show. Why wouldn't Sylvia want her to bond with her baby?

She reached over to switch on the lamp on the end table and the light reflected onto a silver picture frame. Lisette hadn't noticed it before, but Sylvia had placed a five by seven picture of a smiling Roger on that table. She smiled back at her handsome husband. Lisette supposed that Roger would want her to get along with his mother as guilt overwhelmed her.

Sylvia finished up preparing the spaghetti while Lisette fed Rebecca her bottled formula. When the spaghetti was ready, and Rebecca was full, Lisette placed her in her carriage. Sylvia placed their plates on the table along with two glasses of iced tea. Then she sat down and began to eat her spaghetti. After a few quiet moments of chewing and sipping, Sylvia finished her food, pushed her chair back, and took her dirty dishes to the kitchen. Then she headed over to the couch to watch the news without another word to Lisette.

A few minutes later, Lisette finished her own dinner and took her dishes to the kitchen. While she was rinsing the dishes and placing them in the dishwasher, the phone on the kitchen wall rang. She grabbed a bright yellow dish cloth, dried her hands, and walked across the kitchen. "Hello?"

"Lisette, hi. It's David." His voice soothed like a warm compress.

"Hi." A smile formed on Lisette's lips as she spoke.

David got to the point. "Are you free this Saturday?"

"When?"

"The whole afternoon?"

Lisette's forehead crinkled. "Why?"

David laughed. "Would you quit asking questions to my questions?"

"I want to know what's going on." Lisette smirked.

"And I want to take you and Rebecca out for a wonderful afternoon. It's supposed to be a beautiful fall day."

"Where would we go?"

David sighed. "Just leave that to me. I'll plan everything, and it'll be very nice. You'll see."

"But where?"

"Shh. No more questions. I'll pick you two up at about noon. Is that time good?"

Lisette had no real objections, so she relented. "Okay, noon it is."

"You won't regret it." David spoke with a confidence that was very appealing.

Lisette didn't mention anything about Saturday to Sylvia. She wasn't in the mood to hear her objections. She would tell her tomorrow after they both got a good night's sleep and things were...umm...fresher. At least Lisette hoped that things would be better by then. She picked up Rebecca, carried her into her room, and shut the door. Then she put Rebecca into her crib. Rebecca was where she had wanted her to sleep all along.

Then she got out her journal and began to write about her mixed-up bag of feelings.

I'm being selfish, Rebecca. Your grandmother loves you very much. And she has been a great help. I guess I'm just starting to feel like your mother more and more. This has been a big surprise. A year ago, I couldn't imagine my life without Roger. And a few months ago, I couldn't imagine my life with you. But now, I can't imagine being without you. You are my little angel from heaven. The more I'm around you, the more you are healing me. I still don't know if I can handle you full-time, forever but I love you and I think I might want to try.

What am I going to do about David? He knows all I can handle is friendship and I think he's respecting that boundary. However, there's this other part of me that tingles when I hear his voice. That shouldn't be happening but nonetheless it does. Nevertheless, if we're only friends, I don't have to worry about any of that so that's how it will stay. Roger was my everything. It wouldn't be fair to him for me to be happy again with David. Would it?

A teardrop fell onto the paper. Lisette slammed the journal shut. She shouldn't even entertain the thought of anything more than friends with David.

Lisette awoke to Rebecca crying and glanced at the digits on her nightstand. Ten minutes after twelve. She got up, hurried over to the crib, and lifted Rebecca into her arms. "It's okay, Rebecca. Mommy's here."

Rebecca continued to cry. Lisette squeezed a little tighter and rocked her baby. The soft cry turned into a whimper but didn't stop. "I guess, it's time for more formula?"

She carried Rebecca into the living room and laid her in her carriage. Then she glanced over at Sylvia who seemed to be sound asleep. As quietly as she could, she pushed the carriage into the kitchen. Sylvia had her formula schedule posted on the fridge and sure enough twelve o'clock was listed there.

Lisette got a prepared bottle out of the fridge, took off the amber, rubbery nipple and placed the clear, half full bottle into the microwave for thirty seconds. Then she replaced the nipple and shook it to distribute the heat. She wanted to make sure that the formula wasn't too hot, so she held the side of the bottle under a tepid water flow in the sink for a few seconds. She had read it was safer for the formula to be not-warm-enough than to take a chance on it being too hot. When she was satisfied with the temperature, Lisette picked up Rebecca again, sat down on the kitchen chair, and fed her. Rebecca sucked the white liquid vigorously.

Even in her groggy state, the act of feeding her little baby made Lisette smile and forget her worries for a while. At least for a few minutes, everything felt right in the world, even her messed-up one.

Later when Rebecca and she were back in the bedroom Lisette again picked up her journal and wrote:

If it could just be you and me in this room alone for the rest of our lives, it would all be good, Rebecca. But it's not that simple. I must go to work to raise you. There will always be complications. Although, looking at your sweet and innocent face, the complications seem so much less.

CHAPTER 23

David arrived at Lisette's apartment at eleven-thirty on Saturday morning with two coffees in hand. "I got you a mocha coffee. I hope you like it. I also wanted to come early so we could get all of the baby paraphernalia in the car easily."

David would think of things like that. He always seemed to think of everything. Lisette sipped her coffee right away. "Thank you, David, that was very nice of you."

David carried the full diaper bag, along with Lisette's purse, to the car while Lisette only had to carry Rebecca in her carrier. David still had the car seat connector in his car from the day he had picked them up from the hospital, so Lisette attached the carrier to it.

Lisette had on a light jacket. She looked up to a bright blue sky with just a few wispy white clouds then rolled down the window about an inch to feel the cool crispness of the air. The coolness refreshed her, but she was glad that Rebecca had her little pink stocking cap on and was wrapped in her pink blanket.

"David, where are we going?"

David looked at her with that mischievous half-smile. "I can't tell you, but you'll see soon enough. I think you'll like it."

"What?" Lisette proclaimed and then added a mock whine. "Why can't I know now?"

"Because I want it to be a surprise." David winked.

Lisette pretended to look irritated.

"But Rebecca knows. I already told her, and she thinks it's a good idea."

Lisette rolled her eyes as her lips formed a smirk.

"See you're having fun already. I told you."

David's dark blue Camry took them out of the city and up interstate 95. Lisette hadn't been out of the city in over a year. She had been with Roger the last time she had made this trek northward. Roger used to like to take drives to different counties. He didn't love the city but that was where some of the best jobs were. He had always planned to move out to a county as soon as they could afford it.

For a moment, Lisette pictured Roger in David's place in the driver's seat. In a déjà vu feeling, something seemed right. Once again Lisette wondered if she was ever going to stop missing Roger. She blinked multiple times to thwart any possibility of tears falling. The quicker the images faded, the less likely her tears would start flowing again.

After about thirty minutes, David exited 95 onto a road that Lisette didn't recognize. It seemed to lead into the country. Houses became sporadic and trees seemed to multiply. Farms were the normal scenery. Lisette even saw long fields with horses. The leaves were beginning to change into their fall colors but there were still a lot of green leaves. After another ten minutes, David slowed and turned onto a long dirt road.

Lisette read a sign, Welcome to Appleview Farm, as she looked around at lush apple trees, hay bale stacks, and scarecrows. She even saw a pumpkin patch off to the right. Children frolicked all around the vast fields. Childlike enthusiasm showed on Lisette's face as she lifted herself in her seat to get a better look at the idyllic scene all around her. David pulled into a large dirt parking area. There were already four long lines of parked cars in the makeshift parking lot that was just a field.

When the car stopped, and David took the keys out of the ignition, Lisette blurted out, "This looks fun, David. How'd you think of this?"

"Oh, I've come here a lot over the years. It's a great place. They have events in the spring and summer as well, but the fall seems to have its own brand of magic."

They got out of the car and Lisette opened the back door to free Rebecca. She threw the diaper bag and her purse over her shoulder and then bent down to lift the carrier. Rebecca still looked sleepy. Lisette whispered, "Rebecca, this will be a fun day."

David interrupted by tapping Lisette on the shoulder. He reached for the diaper bag and Lisette's purse and put them onto his left shoulder. Lisette didn't know why but it seemed natural for him to release some of her burden. He'd been doing that continually in the short time they'd known each other.

They walked around so David could show Lisette more of the farm. There was a corn maze and a small train that rode on tracks around the pumpkin patch. A large field behind the train tracks had tractor-pulled hayrides. At the center of everything was a combination gift shop and refreshment stand. Picnic tables were placed strategically all around. And there were also pony rides and a petting zoo with small farm animals. As Lisette took in the scene, David smiled. He seemed pleased at her obvious appreciation.

They found an available picnic table and set Rebecca's carrier on one end. David set the diaper bag on the table next to Rebecca and handed her the purse. Lisette sat down on the bench herself and sighed. "It's not as easy to take a walk nowadays. There's too much stuff to carry."

David smiled at her. "You rest for a moment and I'll go get us something to drink. Today is about refreshment and relaxation." With that, David headed for the red wooden barn-like building that housed the refreshment stand and gift shop.

Lisette took in even more of the surrounding scene. Some kids played tag, some ate caramel apples on sticks, and some tried to get as close to where the farm animals were as they could. Next year, Rebecca might enjoy some of it.

Lisette pondered coming back next fall. Then she

shook her head when she realized that she might not even have Rebecca next year. Rebecca could be with a loving whole family. And without Rebecca in the picture she and David might not even be friends. No, there would be no coming back the next year.

David came back with two tall drinks in white Styrofoam cups with lids and straws. "It's apple cider. I hope you like it, Lisette."

"Oh, I love apple cider. I haven't had it in a long time." Lisette took a long sip through her straw and swallowed the sweet nectar. "Yum, thank you."

"No problem. I love this stuff too." David paused, took a sip of his drink, and then spoke again. "They had some purified apple juice that said it was good for young kids, but I thought maybe Rebecca was too young even for that."

"I think I read somewhere that babies don't really need anything but their formula for the first three months or so. You're probably right." Lisette looked up at the bright warm sun. "But if it remains this warm, maybe I should give her some water." Lisette reached into the diaper bag and pulled out a bottle full of water and held it for Rebecca.

Rebecca sipped happily, and Lisette took another sip of her own sweet nectar. Then she spoke, "Umm... David?"

"Yes."

"Umm...you told me about your past. You know... about your wife and baby." Lisette looked down at the cherry red picnic table where someone had carved a peace symbol. She couldn't seem to look

David in his face when she mentioned his past.

"Lisette, you can ask me anything, even about that," David answered.

She breathed fresh, cool, autumn air into her nostrils. "Well...I was just wondering...umm...how you got through it? I mean, you seem well-adjusted now."

"I wasn't always this good at handling it, Lisette. I'll be the first to admit that I was a mess for probably a year or longer. I threw myself into my studies to take my mind off everything. That's all I concentrated on for over a year. My way of handling it became not handling it." David paused. "That's probably why my grades got better afterwards. I was forced into concentration."

"I know how that feels," Lisette muttered. "Doing what you know to do, without thinking too much, just doing."

David continued, "I think God gave me something else to concentrate on, so I wouldn't have as much time to be depressed."

Lisette nodded. "Is that the simple answer? That God got you through?"

"Well, yeah, I think my faith played a big part in my recovery. The bible has a way of putting things into perspective."

"What perspective? That makes it seem like it was a good thing."

"No, Lisette. It wasn't a good thing for my wife and baby to die. And...it wasn't a good thing for your Roger to die. They were both terrible tragedies. But...God can help us get through those things. I know he did for me."

Lisette wondered if she could ever get her faith back.

David seemed to look right through Lisette. "You can trust God again. It may not feel like it now, but you can."

Lisette nodded robotically.

"But Lisette," David began again. "I'm not super-human or anything. I did question God. I wondered why he could let such a terrible thing happen."

Lisette nodded again.

"One night, two weeks after it happened, I knelt in prayer and began praying questions to God. I started off very angry and just listed question after question. I even yelled some of them out loud. However, the further I went along, the more I realized that I may never understand why it happened. Why isn't always the best question to ask. But you know what, Lisette?"

"What?"

"God never left me. He was always there to comfort me. He brought just the right scripture at just the right time when I needed it. He brought just the right people into my life that could comfort me. He even brought situations that made me remember very good times with my wife. My good memories became like gold and I cherished each one. And the more I went on with that perspective, the more I realized that God didn't cause my wife and child to die. It just happened."

Lisette looked directly into David's eyes and asked,

"But what if God let it happen to punish me?"

"God doesn't work like that, Lisette. God is love." David spoke plainly.

"But what if God was mad at me because I had argued with Roger and because of that argument I didn't go with him that night. So, God caused something bad to happen to punish me." She looked away from David and dabbed at her moist eyes.

"Again, that's not how God works, Lisette. Arguments happen. Roger probably forgave you the minute he stepped out the front door. I know that when I argued with Laura, I always forgave her quickly and she forgave me just as quickly. But the argument has nothing to do with the accident, Lisette. The accident just happened. It definitely wasn't in any way your fault."

Lisette heard everything David said but she didn't reply. It was nice to hear it though and maybe in time she could come to believe it.

"But there was another thing crucial to my recovery." David added. "My parents were very supportive. They kind of forced me to talk a little about the tragedy from time to time. They knew I needed to let some steam out or I might have exploded from the pressure."

"Sandra does that for me a lot."

"Doesn't it help...a little?"

Lisette nodded. She didn't tell him that at other times Sandra tried to get her to talk and she would refuse. She didn't want to talk about it all the time.

"How about your parents? Have they been helpful?"

"Well...when it first happened, I talked to my mom a few times on the phone. Dad's in Texas and Mom's in California. I haven't talked to my dad since he left us. My mom showed that she did care about me in her own way but in the first couple of months I was too numb to take in much comfort at all." Lisette continued, "They really haven't been a big part of my life since their divorce."

David nodded. "I understand that in the beginning, it's harder to feel any comfort but each month gets easier and you feel more comfort gradually."

Lisette nodded again.

"Most of all, Lisette, the Lord will get you through. Don't give up praying to him. Even when you don't know what to say, he'll comfort you. He knows what you need before you ask."

Lisette had heard things like that in church for years, but she hadn't felt it personally since Roger died.

"And Lisette, you can talk to me any time you need to talk about it. I'm here to listen. It may be a cliché but that's what friends are for."

She smiled. Cliché or no cliché, lines like that seem to bring healing all by themselves.

David and Lisette grew quiet but continued to sip on their drinks. But it wasn't an uncomfortable silence. It was calming, even peaceful to know David really got her. He understood perfectly. He'd been there. And maybe one day she'd see even more of her situation through his eyes of faith.

When they finished their drinks, they walked over

to the corn maze and decided to try it. They walked slowly. David carried the baby carrier while Lisette made the decisions which way to go. They only had to backtrack two times and they reached the end in about twenty minutes. Then they walked around the pumpkin patch. Some pumpkins in there were about two feet in diameter. Lisette decided to skip the petting zoo area. She didn't want to expose Rebecca to germs.

They walked through the playground where Lisette spied an empty swing. Her mind reverted back to her high school days when Roger and she would take long walks that included a stroll through a playground. Roger would push her on the swing for a while and she would feel as free as a little kid seeing how high they could swing.

"You suddenly started to walk much slower. Are you okay, Lisette?"

She shook her head. "It's nothing. Just lost in my thoughts, I guess."

"You seemed to be looking at that swing. Were you?"

She nodded.

David grinned. "Well, come on. Sit down. I'll push you."

Lisette shook her head again. "No, don't be silly. We're adults."

"What does that matter? Just sit down, Lisette." David ordered pleasantly.

Lisette gave in and set Rebecca's carrier down to the right of the swing in a position where she could see her. Then, against her better judgment, she sat down and grabbed hold of the chains. She pushed off and began to feel the wind.

David moved behind her and began to push gently at first but then he pushed a little harder. Her legs were parallel with the ground and the crisp air freed the strain and worry of her body. She closed her eyes as she pictured Roger pushing her. They had both been carefree and, except for an occasional test in school, they were worry free. She smiled as she remembered those feelings of such grand hope. Hope that Roger and she would be together forever.

She pointed her feet toward the ground and reached down to let the ground stop her flight. The swing jolted to an erratic end as she tried to steady herself to stand up.

"Lisette?" David questioned with concern in his voice.

"Roger?" She absentmindedly spoke.

"Lisette, it's David. Are you okay?"

She turned around to see David's face and it did look concerned." I'm sorry, David, can we head back soon?"

"Sure, Lisette," David's voice was soothing. "Memories again?"

Lisette nodded.

David nodded in return and then he reached down to pick up Rebecca's carrier. "Come on, let's go back."

David gave the impression he saw her erratic actions as normal. Again, he seemed to understand what she was going through.

They made one last stop in the gift shop where David insisted on buying her a jar of apple butter, a container of pumpkin butter, and a gallon of apple cider. He told her that all three of those things are the best he'd had. She took Rebecca into the restroom to change her diaper before the car ride home.

The car ride home took fifty minutes and was solemn. When they arrived back in front of Lisette's apartment building, Lisette fumbled for her keys as she noticed that it was only five-thirty. The afternoon had flown by. "Thank you for a wonderful afternoon, David. I had a good time."

"You're welcome. It was my pleasure. I always enjoy it there."

Lisette pointed to the backseat and smiled. "I think if Rebecca could speak, she'd say it was a fun outing too."

"Yeah, she'll have to see it later when she's old enough to understand what she's seeing."

"It's still early, David, and we haven't had dinner. Would you want to come up and we could order Chinese or something?" It seemed fair to Lisette to reciprocate David's kindness by offering a kindness of her own. She didn't want to admit it, but Lisette didn't want this day to end so soon.

David smiled. "That would be nice, Lisette. But will Sylvia mind? She doesn't always seem like the happiest person."

"David, it's my place. I can have a friend over for dinner if I want." Lisette's upper body straightened and stiffened as she spoke.

David chuckled at Lisette's obvious annoyance. "Of course you can. Let me pull into that garage next door then."

He found a parking spot on the first level of the garage and they began to gather their things. David opened the back door and leaned over the backseat to unhook Rebecca's carrier as Lisette waited at the front of the car. She overheard him making cute baby talk banter to Rebecca, and it made her smile. Then she almost choked on her own saliva when she heard him make a Donald Duck type voice to Rebecca. It sounded just like the voice Roger used to make.

They ate a Chinese dinner on Lisette's dining room table with Sylvia watching television in the adjoining living room. It felt like they had a chaperone. Lisette had asked Sylvia if she wanted to join them, but Sylvia replied with a curt, "No, thank you, I'm fine with my salad."

After dinner, Lisette walked David to the front door and stepped out into the hallway with him. They couldn't extend their evening anymore by watching something on television because Sylvia had control of it.

"Thanks for dinner, Lisette."

"No, thank you, dinner was nothing. The rest of the

day was fantastic."

"You're welcome again then."

Lisette couldn't take her eyes off David's warm smile. Before she had time to object, he leaned over and kissed her on the mouth. Even though it caught Lisette off guard, it felt natural. Lisette even kissed back a little. It was a short and sweet kiss and seemed like the normal thing to do at the end of a successful date. Lisette raised her right finger tips to cover her mouth. "David, I thought we were just friends?"

David looked down at the maroon carpet under his feet trying to hide his embarrassment. "I'm sorry, Lisette. I really am. But, honestly, that just felt right to do. I had a wonderful time today." As David spoke, his eyes lifted from the floor to her eyes.

"But friends don't kiss like that, not with that kind of electricity," Lisette stammered.

David smiled again then, "Electricity?"

Lisette almost stuttered. "I didn't mean to say that."

"But you said it." David was still grinning.

"Okay, okay, I felt something. All right? What do you want from me?"

David set both of his hands on Lisette's shoulders. His gentle touch calmed her trembling. "I want to get to know you better. I like you...a lot." David bent down and brushed his lips against Lisette's again but this time he pressed into the kiss longer.

Lisette wanted to object but didn't. She found herself kissing back. The electricity from before was real.

David ended the kiss by pulling back but kept his

gaze focused on Lisette's face. Lisette didn't say a word. She didn't think she could.

He took a few steps backward and finally spoke again. "Good night, Lisette."

Lisette lifted her right hand up slowly and gave a little wave as she managed to whisper a meek, "Bye."

CHAPTER 24

L isette sat at the kitchen table trying to keep her eyes open. A barely touched bowl of soggy raisin bran cereal sat in front of her. Rebecca had fallen into a routine of feeding about every three hours and it was exhausting. Lisette supposed that all new mothers must get used to fragmented sleep, at least she hoped they did. Some of her sleeplessness was getting up with Rebecca but most of it was deciphering her feelings for David.

David was a great guy and he cared for both her and Rebecca, and Rebecca wasn't even his responsibility. What kind of guy did that so readily? Her Roger would have. Of course, that was the real problem. Lisette couldn't get passed her guilt over Roger. Shame filled her for even thinking about the possibility.

Sylvia walked into the kitchen and interrupted Lisette's thoughts. With a straight face and no trace of a smile, she said, "Good morning."

"Good morning," Lisette echoed.

Sylvia reached into the top cabinet and pulled out

her oat bran cereal. After preparing her breakfast, Sylvia sat down at the table.

Lisette stirred her own cereal and forced herself to take a few bites of the soggy mess.

After Sylvia swallowed her first bite, she looked up and spoke, "I have to say something."

Lisette's forehead crinkled. "Huh?"

"Yesterday, you spent the whole day with that David fellow."

"Yeah, so?" Lisette was having enough trouble of her own worrying about that matter. She didn't want to hear Sylvia's two cents.

"Are you serious about him?"

"No." Lisette burst out.

"Well, you have another little person to worry about now. Your life isn't just about you anymore." Sylvia's face was stern with contempt.

"I am taking care of Rebecca. She was with me." Lisette wrung her hands in front of her stomach. "And, by the way, it's never been just about me. It was always me and Roger for a long time."

"Be careful about the company you keep now."

Lisette couldn't believe the indignation that was spewing from Sylvia's mouth. She knew nothing about David. Lisette took a deep breath to calm herself down. "David is very nice. We're friends. What's wrong with that?"

"I see the way he looks at you. And it's not the look of just a friend."

"That's my business, not yours." Lisette defended David. He was a perfect gentleman. If anything, he was too nice, but that's nothing to find fault with. "Not only is he a friend, but he's showed himself to be kind and helpful to Rebecca."

Sylvia continued to glare at Lisette. "Lisette, why would this man be so interested in another man's baby?"

"He's a nice guy who cares about me and Rebecca." Lisette's voice kept going up in volume. Instantly, a picture of a downtrodden David when he told her of his own tragic past popped into her head.

"Lisette, I'm only trying to help you." Sylvia tried to calm the heat of the conversation by slowing and quieting her voice. "What would Roger think of this? He hasn't even been gone a year yet." Sylvia's dark blue eyes looked watery.

"Roger would want me to be happy," Lisette whimpered, trying to emulate Sandra's words. Somehow, they sounded more convincing coming out of Sandra's mouth than her own.

"With another man?"

Sylvia was stepping on Lisette's last nerve now. Didn't she realize how she had agonized over all of this? How much she had mourned? How empty she had become? "But...Roger's not here." Tears started to squirt out of Lisette's eyes.

"But, Lisette, his baby is here."

"I'm trying, I really am," Lisette whimpered again. "This whole thing has been excruciatingly hard on me. Who are you to belittle my pain?"

Sylvia reached for Lisette's hand and rubbed it a little too hard. Lisette pulled her hand away.

"I know. I know you're trying, dear, and I'm wanting to continue to help you. We'll be okay. We'll get through this. Just you, me, and Rebecca. We'll preserve Roger's memory by sticking together."

Lisette sniffed and wiped at both cheeks to dry them. "You're staying? Here?"

"Of course, I'll help you with Rebecca." Sylvia stiffened her upper body and pulled her shoulders back.

"I thought you were just getting me through my recovery from surgery and the initial learning stage with Rebecca."

Sylvia forced a smile. "You need my help longer, Lisette."

"You've been a great help, Sylvia, but I always thought this was just a temporary arrangement."

"You don't want me here?" A haughty and lonesome tone emerged from Sylvia's lips.

"I said you were a great help, Sylvia."

"But you don't want me to stay."

Lisette shook her head, not believing what she heard. "Sylvia, what about Louis? Your husband?"

"Louis hasn't needed me for a long time. He's perfectly fine by himself."

"So, you want to live apart from Louis permanently?"

Sylvia shrugged one shoulder. "He doesn't care."

"Your husband doesn't care?"

"Ever since Roger died, we haven't talked much, Lisette," Sylvia spoke matter-of-factly but Lisette saw worry and even sadness in the squint of her eyes.

"But don't you need to help each other through this

tragedy? He's probably hurting just as much as you."

"No." Sylvia shook her head. "I'll stay here with you and he'll be fine. Men can get through these things better than women."

"Sylvia, you can't do that." A fire rose from Lisette's belly. "Like you said, Roger wouldn't want that. He would want his parents to be happy and living together."

Sylvia's face turned crimson. Her eyes glistened and gasping sobs escaped her mouth.

Lisette didn't know what to do. She had never seen Sylvia out-of-control like this.

But Sylvia's sobs didn't slow down. In fact, they got worse until she slid her cereal bowl to the side and buried her face in her folded arms.

Lisette reached over and rubbed Sylvia's shoulder slowly, back and forth.

"I thought..." a muffled sound emerged from under Sylvia's arms.

"Yes?" Lisette answered.

Sylvia's face remained buried. "I thought...that being around little Rebecca would heal my broken heart."

"Sylvia, I want you to see Rebecca. I want you to be a grandma to her and see her regularly."

"I guess I was wrong." Sylvia continued as if Lisette hadn't said anything, "Being around little Rebecca has been wonderful and I've enjoyed it very much but...it's not healing my broken heart over...my son. Rebecca is great but she's not my Roger. I want my son back." Her sobs grew stronger.

Lisette hadn't realized just how deep Sylvia's grief still was. But of course, it was. Just like her own. It seemed to not have an end. Couldn't God see the heartache that two women would endure after this one man's passing?

"Hello Lisette." David's cheerful voice spoke through the phone. "I got out of church and noticed that it is another beautiful fall day. I thought you and Rebecca might want to go to a park or something."

"Uhh...I can't."

"Oh," David's cheerful tone deflated. "Well, that's okay. I probably shouldn't have called you at the last minute like this."

Lisette didn't want David to call now. Not after her latest conversation with Sylvia. But how could she tell him about this new revelation?

Many seconds went by with no response from Lisette.

"Lisette, are you okay?"

Lisette sucked in a breath and held it for three seconds. A dose of courage seemed to overtake her. "I am okay...David. You didn't do anything wrong. I...umm...just don't want to go anywhere." Lisette took another deep breath and continued. "Anywhere...ever...with you."

Lisette knew she had to be direct after what happened yesterday and after what happened with Sylvia. She couldn't see David ever again even as a friend.

It was just not right.

"Okay, I'm sorry to have bothered you."

David's voice sounded like Lisette's harsh words had poked multiple holes in his gut.

Lisette felt very guilty and something closer to her regular voice came out. "Uh...that's okay, David."

"No, I've bothered you enough, Lisette. I'll let you go now. Bye." With that, David hung up.

Well, that was the end of that. She had fixed it.

However, even if it was right to end it with David, she had done it in a terrible way. Out of the blue like that? And so mean?

Lisette wanted to call him back and apologize for her rudeness. But maybe it was better this way. It was done. Now, he could go on and find some other woman that can treat him as good as he deserved. She had yanked the Band-Aid off before it could hurt too much for either one of them.

But if it was so right why did Lisette feel a deep sting?

That night, she sat on the edge of her bed staring at that little fuchsia book. Maybe it wasn't such a good idea to start writing in it. Sure, it had helped to get things out but now she heard David's assuring voice when she opened it.

Sometimes thoughts and feelings need to stay buried inside. Getting them out only gets you into trouble. Lisette opened the second drawer of her nightstand and buried the book under some other books. Then she shut the drawer.

CHAPTER 25

Lisette called Sandra the next day to tell her what had happened in the David situation. Sandra's disappointment couldn't be hidden.

"Lisette, why?" Sandra blurted out.

Lisette held the phone and lifted her legs up into a crossed legged position on the middle of her bed but didn't speak a word. The lament in Sandra's voice made her wonder if she had made a mistake. But didn't she have to end everything with David, even friendship, for the sake of Roger's memory? Roger deserved at least that much.

"Oh, I am sorry, Lisette." Sandra attempted to sound soothing. "I know how hard this whole thing has been on you. I don't want to make it any harder by adding more guilt. I'm sorry."

"It has been hard." Lisette admitted. She couldn't preserve Roger's memory and be David's friend at the same time.

"Maybe this is for the best then. Maybe it's just not the right timing," Sandra relented as she spoke with a very uncharacteristic desolate tone.

Lisette wondered if maybe she was finally giving up on the whole David idea. "I did what I had to do, Sandra."

"I'm not, Lisette. I said I was sorry. I never wanted you to feel guilty." Sandra defended herself.

"You feel sorry for me. The poor girl that can't fall in love again. The poor girl who can't recover from a mishap." Lisette was again surprised by the mean-spirited tone that seemed to flow out of her.

"No, no, Lisette. What you went through is far worse than a mishap. I never meant to belittle it."

"Yes, it is. You don't know what it's like, Sandra. You don't know how terrible I feel. Why don't you mind your own business?" Lisette continued her tirade. Something had to give. She couldn't take the pressure anymore. Everyone was pushing and pushing. "And...if you know so much about love...then where's your husband? Why aren't you married?" Lisette knew she was hurting Sandra, but she didn't care.

"I'm sorry." Sandra repeated, her voice not much more than a quiver. "You're right, I'm not married so I don't know how you're feeling."

"Good. Maybe this will teach you a lesson. To stay out of other people's business. You don't know what it was like with me and Roger. You don't know how much I've grieved. You just don't know, Sandra."

"I...I...I tried to understand. I...I tried to listen. I tried to be your friend, that's all," Sandra whimpered.

"I didn't ask for any of that, Sandra."

Sandra grew so quiet that Lisette wondered if she

had hung up.

"Sandra, are you there?" She asked half-expecting no one to answer.

"Yes, I'm still here, Lisette, but I should probably go. I've caused you enough problems."

"Good, at least you realize that now."

"Goodbye, Lisette. I...really am sorry."

Lisette didn't hear anything else after that. The conversation was over, along with her and Sandra's friendship.

David was gone from her life.

Now, Sandra was too.

Everything was falling apart. It made sense that things would continue to fall apart because her life had ended the day Roger died. Nothing else was supposed to happen to her. She wasn't supposed to live after that point so now everything else was crumbling down around her.

Lisette rubbed her forehead where a headache was beginning. Then she picked up her cell phone again to call her mom. She didn't know what she wanted to say to her mom but supposed that she wanted to hear her voice.

It rang but there was no answer. Her mom's voice mail message came on. "Hi, I'm probably out with Bill and I'm deliriously happy right now so leave a message and I'll get back to you as soon as I can," her voice chirped.

"Umm...hi, mom...it's me, Lisette, I guess I called to talk to you. See how you've been. Your voice mail message sounds like you're happy. I'm glad. Well, call me when you get a chance. Bye."

Lisette wondered if Bill was the same guy she was having a first date with at the end of August. It hadn't been that long, but she said she was deliriously happy. Lisette sighed and hoped she wasn't setting herself up for another fall, like all the other ones. Ever since the divorce, Lisette always felt like she was the mother when she talked to her mom. She sighed again and hoped that Rebecca would never think of her like that.

The next few weeks dragged by.

Many times, Lisette wondered if she should call Sandra and apologize but then she changed her mind. Sandra didn't have to be so relentless with her crazy notions. Lisette also wondered if she should try to find another job. She wasn't looking forward to going back to the diner and facing Sandra. Deep down, Lisette knew Sandra hadn't meant any harm. But she had made her feel guilty about David. It was good that both were out of her life.

Over the next few weeks, Lisette went through the motions of continuing to learn how to care for Rebecca. She felt she might be getting good at it. Rebecca was the light that was getting her through these dark times.

Lisette had always been good at throwing herself into whatever had to get done. It was a good way to live. Just do what was expected, no more and no less, and you get by just fine.

Sylvia fit in well with the new lifestyle Lisette had adopted. She did whatever was needed when it was needed. Rebecca was being looked after. The meals were being cooked. The house cleaning was getting done. They were both doing just fine.

Then there were the times when everything was done, Rebecca was sleeping, and they both sat there in the dimly lit living room with the television on. That was when something just didn't feel right.

Lisette was grateful for the television's sounds. They provided a numbing relief for her brain. It was nice. It seemed that numbness had been Lisette's chosen way to cope ever since Thanksgiving weekend almost a year ago. She didn't know why people tended to think of numbness as a bad thing. It was comfortable. It was like wrapping yourself up in a big, protective cocoon.

The only thing Lisette was thankful for was Rebecca. She was very thankful for her little baby. Maybe she would spend extra time on Thanksgiving weekend snuggling with her baby. What if she didn't have her much longer? What if she started an adoption plan? She should enjoy her as much as possible until then.

Lisette knew her mantra of getting by was a good one. It had been working for almost a year now. But what if she was wrong?

What if she collapsed from the pressure?

CHAPTER 26

L isette reached for her jacket in the front closet. "Sylvia, will you be okay with Rebecca while I go outside and take a walk?"

Sylvia looked up from her book. "Of course, me and Rebecca will be just fine. She was sound asleep the last time I looked in on her. She's such a good baby."

Lisette nodded. "Yes, she is." She opened the front door and stepped into the hallway.

The chilly, dusk air felt refreshing to Lisette as she walked toward the inner harbor area. It seemed like many people were out enjoying the nice fall weather before winter set in.

So many thoughts had been running through her mind for weeks. She needed to get outside for a fresh perspective.

Her first problem was what to do with Rebecca. She loved her dearly but still was not sure she'd be able to take care of her by herself. Even if she could get by on her own, would it be the best thing for Rebecca? Wouldn't she be happier with a real family that had both a mommy and a daddy and maybe even a brother or sister? Yes, Rebecca deserved the best.

The next problem weighing her down was David. Maybe it had been the right thing to end everything with him, but did she have to do it the way she did it? David deserved more than that.

Then there was Sandra. She cared for Lisette and had only meant to help her. They were dear friends. Sandra didn't deserve to be treated badly either.

Why did she keep treating others so badly?

The inner harbor area was very crowded for a fall evening. Lisette had hoped for a quieter atmosphere. She sat down on the edge of the walkway. Her feet dangled about three feet above the water.

Why didn't her mom want anything to do with her? Why was her love life so much more important than her daughter? She hadn't been a part of Lisette's life for years but sometimes a girl just wanted her mom.

All around Lisette were tainted relationships. Her parents' divorce. An argument with Roger that may have led to his death. Yelling at her best friend in the whole wide world who had been nothing but kind to her. And dismissing a man with a hurting past like he was nothing. What was wrong with her?

She sat there for quite a while. Her mind grew blank. She didn't know what to do about anything.

Lisette noticed the crowd had dissipated. It was now dusk and quiet.

She went back to staring at the murky water.

The local news periodically reported on people

that had fallen into the water and drowned. It would be easy to drown in here because the ledge was so high and there was not much to grab a hold of if you fell in. You would just quietly sink to the bottom. It might even feel peaceful. No more worries.

Lisette wondered. Could she dare?

No one liked her now anyway. No one would miss her. Even Rebecca was too young to remember her. Sylvia would bring her home and her and Louis would take care of their grandbaby. Yes, Rebecca would be just fine.

Lisette wondered.

She scooted a few inches closer to the edge.

And maybe she'd see Roger again instantly.

She smiled.

Then she scooted a few more inches closer.

Her knuckles were holding the ledge and they were turning white.

She started to push herself even closer. It wouldn't be long now. She wouldn't be able to hold much longer.

She closed her eyes and whispered, "Bye."

Lisette felt strong hands gripping her armpits and was lifted straight up and away from the edge. When she was set down on the brick ground, her knees gave way and she collapsed. She looked up at a very tall man she didn't recognize.

"Are you okay?" The man's voice boomed.

"Yes." Lisette's voice was audibly shaken.

The man helped her to her feet. "There's a bench over there. You can rest a moment."

Lisette realized the magnitude of what she almost did. "No...no...I need to go home."

"Umm...miss...you're not okay. Just sit down for a few minutes."

"No...I...I...got to go." She gasped for more air as sobs came.

"Please, just sit a minute...just until you recover."

Lisette realized that in the shape she was in, she'd probably get hit by a car or something if she tried to go home right then. And now she realized that she did not want to kill herself. At least not anymore. She was scared as she investigated the stranger's face.

The man smiled and led her to a bench where they both sat down. Lisette took another good look at the man. He seemed to be in his forties or maybe fifties. He was tall, wide, and rather burly which explained why he could lift Lisette so adeptly. His salt and pepper hair looked distinguished.

Lisette finally let the words, "Thank you" come out of her mouth.

The man nodded and gave a slight smile. "You must have been deep in thought, young lady."

She nodded. Did he know she was thinking of jumping in to that murky water?

The man held his right hand out toward Lisette. "Hi, I'm Sam Spielman."

Lisette took hold of his hand loosely. "I'm Lisette Carter."

"Hi Lisette. Are you really all right?"

He gave Lisette a sort of knowing look like he knew what she had been thinking. She gulped.

"Umm...I...I...guess I'm...umm...okay now."

"Good." Sam paused a few seconds then began again. "I was walking by and talking on my cell phone to my wife when something made me look closely in your direction. At first, I thought there was nothing wrong and I was about to continue. But then I saw you moving slightly toward the edge. It seemed deliberate."

Lisette looked at her lap. She remembered wondering what it would be like to go under the water and never come up.

"I looked again and again and thought something isn't right. I quickly told my wife I'd call her back and then ran toward you."

"Umm...thank you again," was all that Lisette could think of to say.

The man shook his head. "I knew something was wrong and I needed to move fast."

"You did...umm...thank you," Lisette repeated.

"You really don't have to keep saying thank you. I wanted to make sure you were okay."

Lisette saw deep concern in his eyes.

"You're probably not far from my daughter's age and if she was in trouble, I would want someone to help her."

Lisette felt words in her throat that needed to come out. "I am troubled, sir. My husband died almost a year ago. Then I found out I was pregnant. Pregnant and alone. I had the baby a couple months ago. She's beautiful. But I'm scared. And then I yelled at my best friend. My parents aren't anywhere where they can help me. Sylvia's trying to take over my life. And David...David is so sweet and nice, but I yelled at him. I'm ruining everything in my life. Just add me into the mix and all kinds of trouble happens. I deserve nothing good." Tears began to run down Lisette's face.

The man picked up Lisette's left hand and held it. "It does sound like you've been through a lot but that doesn't mean you don't deserve anything good."

"But...but...I can't handle all of this pressure. I can't do it. I don't know what to do. It's too much and I'm too young. Roger would know what to do. He always knew what to do. But he's gone. The best thing in my life and he's gone."

"Roger was your husband that died?" The man spoke like a counselor.

"Yes." Tears continued to flow down Lisette's cheeks.

"Well, that is a terrible thing to happen to a young woman, losing your husband. It's not fair."

"I know. It's not. And I don't think I can go on without him."

"You are wrong about that, Lisette. You can go on. It won't be easy, but you can do it." Then he released hold of her hand and pointed toward her nose. "You. You are still living, Lisette. And you can go on. You can do it. But Lisette?"

"What?"

"You can only do it one step at a time, not all at once. One step at a time. One day at a time. That's all you can handle."

"One step?"

The man nodded. "You can't get through a tragedy any other way."

It sounded too simple and yet it was looking too far forward that always made her anxious and afraid. Maybe there was something to that simple philosophy?

"And Lisette?"

"What?"

"You can do it. You're alive. You're stronger than you think." The man smiled. "And God is even stronger than that. Lean on him as you go."

Lisette tried to smile back as she wiped tear streaks from her cheeks.

The man continued, "He is the Father of mercies and God of all comfort, who comforts us in all our afflictions, so we may be able to comfort those who are in similar afflictions."

Lisette looked up at the man. His dark blue eyes seemed to sparkle under the light from the street lamp. "I used to believe that," Lisette told him.

"Used to?" The man looked at her but not in a judging way. He looked concerned.

"That belief kind of went away from me," Lisette whispered.

"When Roger died?"

She nodded.

The man nodded in return. Then he added, "It only felt like God left you then, but he didn't. The same God that you used to believe in is still here." The man pointed at Lisette's chest. "He is still with you."

"Then why did he take Roger from me?" Lisette earnestly hoped that this wise man could answer that question for her.

"I really don't think God took him. It's just that bad things happen, unfortunately. But...God is there to comfort the people who are left. He helps them to go on. He helps them to live despite the tragedy."

"Like David?"

The man squinted, "Who's David?"

"David is my friend. Well, was my friend. He lost both a wife and a baby a few years ago and God got him through it. He seems so strong now."

"That's what I was saying earlier. God comforts us so we can therefore go out and comfort others." The man smiled like he found a key piece to a jigsaw puzzle. Then he continued, "Someone like that just might be the right person to help you be able to go on. He's been where you are now. It wasn't the same situation, but it was eerily similar. That's the connections that God makes."

Lisette nodded even though she wasn't sure what this man was trying to tell her. Was he telling her that David could be crucial to her life?

The man continued, "This person could help you work through your worries but so can a lot of other people. Friends, relatives, bosses, co-workers, anyone you have a relationship with. God will bring multiple channels of connections to help you. However, you must be open to the help."

"Or even someone I'm just talking to, a stranger, like you?"

The man smiled humbly. "Well, yes, I hope that our talk is helping you."

"I think it has." Lisette was wondering if maybe God sent her the right help at just the right time. If nothing else, she was not on the bottom of the inner harbor right now. This stranger did save her life.

He smiled again and as if reading her mind, he offered another piece of wisdom. "But most of all keep on praying to God. He loves you. And he's the one who is bringing those other helpful people into your life. Keep paying attention."

They wrap up their conversation with Sam giving her his business card. Lisette thanked him again for taking the time to help her.

She was just about to turn to go when Sam added, "Oh...one more thing...whatever you do...don't give up on life. It's precious in your little baby. But it's also precious within you. God loves you."

Lisette smiled as she walked back to her apartment briskly. She longed to see Rebecca in the worst way. That little baby was also an important part of her healing and now she knew she could never give her up.

Lisette also hoped that those other important people still wanted to be a part of her life.

CHAPTER 27

Thanksgiving weekend began like any other weekend. Shouldn't something significant and unusual happen on monumental days?

On Saturday, Sylvia and Lisette ate breakfast with only obligatory remarks as conversation. Lisette assumed that Sylvia had been dreading this time too.

Lisette took a shower and then bathed Rebecca. After that, she went into the living room where Sylvia was watching a morning news program. At the top of the next hour, the anchor news woman mentioned the time and the date. The news woman said it so nonchalantly, like it was any other day. Sylvia and Lisette both looked at each other with empty expressions on their faces. Sylvia snatched up the remote and began punching the channel up button. Lisette watched the pictures come and go.

"There's got to be something else on," Sylvia muttered during her frantic search.

Sylvia's switching channels grated on Lisette's nerves.

"Just put it on anything, Sylvia. Maybe the Food Network or something," Lisette remarked a little too harshly.

Sylvia found the Food Network and stopped.

Lisette settled in to hear about making cookies for the upcoming Christmas season. She knew there would be no cookie baking this season. Lisette was returning to work on the first Monday in December and she didn't even know if she'd be ready for that, much less the Christmas season.

Lisette continued to listen to the brunette woman with the ponytail tied in a red ribbon. Her apron was the same color as her ribbon. She went on and on about ginger cookies, sugar cookies, molasses cookies, chocolate chip cookies, and even colorful, iced Christmas tree cookies. The advice was fine for people who were in the mood to celebrate.

"Maybe I'll make cookies for us this week," Sylvia mused out loud.

"Do you think that will help, Sylvia?"

Sylvia winced at the sudden sarcasm as if Lisette had hit her. "Huh?"

"Cookies aren't going to make us less sad or less lonely, Sylvia." Lisette stared at Sylvia's stunned expression.

"Are you sad, Lisette?" Sylvia looked as if she didn't know what she was talking about.

How could she not know?

"Me?" Lisette questioned and then added, "We're both sad, Sylvia. Pathetically sad, really. We sit around doing nothing and ignoring the giant elephant in the room."

"Elephant?" Sylvia was still staring at her with wild, vacant eyes.

"We tip toe all around each other trying to avoid speaking of our memories of Roger. Sylvia, it's the Saturday after Thanksgiving. Do you know what that means?"

Sylvia blinked multiple times. "Yes, I know what that means, Lisette." She continued. "But I wanted to skip this day or at least ignore it now that it's here."

When Sylvia looked up for a moment, Lisette saw the same sadness in her eyes she was feeling in her heart. "It's the anniversary of the day my beautiful baby boy was taken from me." Sylvia wiped her eyes and then continued. "I can't believe it's been a whole year."

Lisette gulped, sorry for her forcefulness. "I did too. I wanted to ignore the day too. But I don't know if I can."

"Well then." Sylvia wiped at her eyes which now gleamed with determination. "If that's what we both want to do, we can just ignore this day. A few mindless television shows and maybe a movie and this day will be gone."

Lisette knew the elephant couldn't be ignored that easily, but it might be nice to go back to pretending it could.

They both managed to keep up the charade for the next few hours. They watched snippets of people making food. Then they change the channel and watched houses being made over. Finally, Sylvia turned to Lifetime to see if there was a good movie on. One was beginning about a woman scorned getting revenge. This had nothing to do with their own lives, so they agreed to watch it.

◆ ◆ ◆

Halfway through the movie, Lisette's mind kept rambling about the argument that Roger and she had just about a year ago.

"Don't you want to come with me, Lisette?" Roger had asked Lisette.

Lisette remembered glaring at him. "You spring this on me at the last minute and then expect me to just drop everything and go to your parent's house with you. Why didn't you tell me about it yesterday or even this morning?"

"I forgot."

"Well, just pretend that I forgot to go with you." Lisette spewed.

And...Roger left to go to his parent's house.

Roger's only excuse was that he forgot. That's normal. He was human. It seemed so petty now that she had been so angry with him.

Lisette reached over to the coffee table and pressed the mute button on the remote. Sylvia looked at her.

"Sylvia, can I tell you something?" she asked.

Sylvia nodded.

"A year ago, me and Roger had an argument. A stupid argument. And because of that, I didn't go with him when he left for your house."

A rare glimpse of pure empathy showed on Sylvia's face.

"Oh Lisette, you've been thinking Roger's accident was your fault?"

"Well...sort of...if we hadn't argued, maybe things would have worked out differently?" Lisette lamented.

Sylvia paused and then took a deep breath. "A year ago, I was the one who insisted that Roger come to my house. I needed him to go through some of the stuff in his old room. I had insisted that it had to be that weekend." Sylvia sniffed. "So, you see if the accident was anyone's fault, it was mine."

They had both taken on at least partial blame for Roger's accident and that guilt had plagued both for an entire year. And it didn't even seem to make sense now. It wasn't either of their faults. It just happened.

"Sylvia, I think we both need to lift this heavy burden of guilt off our heads or it will kill us."

"I think you're right, Lisette."

In another uncharacteristic move, Sylvia leaned over and gave Lisette a tight hug. Lisette hugged Sylvia back. They stayed that way for a few minutes. Holding and consoling one another.

"Just sharing what we were both thinking has helped a lot. I think it's better to share than to ignore." Lisette spoke as they released their embrace.

"I think you're right, Lisette."

The intercom buzzer caused Lisette and Sylvia to jump when it gave off a shrill ring.

Lisette got up, walked over, and pressed the button. "Hello?"

"Lisette? It's Louis. Can I come up?"

Lisette recognized the gruff voice of her father-in-law instantly. "Yes, Louis, come on up." She pressed the front door release button. She then looked toward Sylvia who looked like a frightened little girl.

A few moments later, Louis came into the apartment. Lisette hugged him. She remembered his many friendly bear hugs while she was dating Roger. He wasn't excessively overweight, but he had a rounded tummy that served to make his hugs softer. Louis was a friendly, jovial, and a comforting man. Roger had taken after his persona.

"Did you come to see your granddaughter?" Lisette asked with a smile.

"I want to see her but that's not why I came. I mainly came to get my wife." He looked over at Sylvia who had hunkered down into the couch cushions, like she was endeavoring to disappear into it. "Sylvia, when are you coming home?"

"I've told you that over the phone, Louis. I'm needed here."

"You can still help Lisette, Sylvia," Louis began in a straightforward, no nonsense tone. "But I want you home. Our home."

"Lisette needs me," Sylvia reiterated and then added, "and Rebecca does too. I need to stay."

Louis walked over toward Sylvia, sat down close to her, and touched her cheek. His voice mellowed as he methodically spoke, "Sylvia, I need you too."

Lisette felt like a fly on the wall watching this loving exchange.

"You do?" Sylvia questioned while angling her body to face her husband.

"I do, Sylvia. I love you. I lost my son. I can't lose my wife too."

"But Louis, we haven't been able to really talk since..." Sylvia's voice trailed off but then she took a breath and could continue, "since a year ago today."

Louis wrapped his arms around his wife. "I know...I know...I didn't want to talk about Roger, so I also didn't have a real conversation with you. I was wrong, Sylvia. I'm sorry. I'm so sorry." Then he paused and loosened his grip on Sylvia, so he could turn his head to face Lisette. "And I also didn't want to talk to you, Lisette, because I didn't want to remember Roger. I'm sorry to you too. I think I was thinking that if I ignored my pain, I would heal. But that didn't work at all."

Lisette walked around and sat in the chair across from them. "That's okay, Louis, we were all deeply hurt. And, we were all afraid to talk about it. That approach didn't help any of us."

Louis loosened his grip on Sylvia and rubbed the top of his legs with his palms a few times. Then his voice got stronger with each word he spoke. "We've all been good at being silent and it hasn't helped any of us heal. But today is the first day of a new year. We've wasted a year in our wallowing. Maybe it was necessary. Maybe it was too much. I don't know which, but I woke up this morning with Roger's face in my brain. And...he was smiling. He wasn't wallowing, and he wouldn't want us to either."

"You're right." Lisette meekly agreed. She didn't think she had ever seen Roger wallow over anything.

"We're all going to begin living again for Roger's sake and for our own sakes. We will talk about Roger any time we need to and in sharing our memories, we'll be sharing life with each other." Louis looked satisfied.

Lisette wanted to share in his satisfaction. She really did. It was an excellent speech. She looked over at Sylvia and wondered if she was having trouble sharing Louis' new philosophy too.

Louis looked back and forth at both ladies. "I thought you'd both need more convincing." He reached into his pocket and pulled out a folded piece of paper. "The last few months I've had a lot of time to think since my wife has been gone." He looked at Sylvia and Sylvia looked shyly downward. "Anyway, I've been looking through Roger's college papers. I'm glad we didn't throw them away, Sylvia, because I found this among them." He held up the folded piece of paper.

"What's that?" Lisette burst out.

"Yeah, what is it, dear?" Sylvia added with the same amount of eagerness.

"I found this among his senior year college papers. He probably wrote it during the last year of his life,"

Louis began.

Lisette saw a tear glistening in Louis's right eye, but it stayed in place. She braced herself and closed her eyes to hear from her late husband.

"For everything there is a season, a time for every activity under heaven. A time to be born and a time to die. A time to plant and a time to harvest. A time to kill and a time to heal. A time to tear down and a time to build up. A time to cry and a time to turn away. A time to search and a time to quit searching. A time to keep and a time to throw away. A time to tear and a time to mend. A time to be quiet and a time to speak. A time to love and a time to hate. A time for war and a time for peace."

Lisette recognized that time-honored passage from the bible and smiled.

Louis continued reading. "Indeed, there is a season for everything, Lord, and I have tried to make the most of my seasons. I try to encourage my parents. I try to encourage my girlfriend. I even try to encourage acquaintances I may never see again. I probably haven't done it perfectly, Lord, and only time will tell if you are happy with how I spent my life but until then I'll continue encouraging people."

Both Sylvia and Lisette smiled at that. Roger had described himself to a tee. Lisette remembered the multitudes of times that Roger had made her smile. He had always encouraged her.

Louis broke into Lisette's wistfulness. "There's more. Do you two want me to continue?"

Sylvia jumped in first. "Of course, go on."

Lisette nodded vigorously.

Louis sucked in an unusual amount of air as if he was gathering his courage to continue. "If I don't have much longer on this earth..."

Lisette raised her hand to cover her mouth.

Louis breathed in and repeated, "If I don't have much longer on this earth." Then he continued Roger's words. "I would like people to know life is a precious gift given by God and I want to use mine well. I want to enjoy it and not take it for granted. If I don't have much longer on this earth, Lord, help me live for others and help meet their needs before my own. Help me remember that you are a God of love and I should be an imitator of that love to people. Thank you for showing me the way."

Louis held up the piece of paper then. "That's it."

Lisette held her hand tighter around her mouth.

"Does that mean he sensed he didn't have much time left?" Sylvia ventured.

"That's a possibility, dear, but it could just be that God gave him a special view of the brevity of life, in general. We should all learn to number our days and live them well. Maybe Roger was an expert in that." Louis spoke with the confidence of a seasoned preacher.

"And it sounds like Roger wouldn't want us to wallow," Sylvia added.

Lisette remembered Sylvia's and her earlier conversation. "No, Roger wouldn't want any of us to wallow."

"No." Louis shook his head. "He would not."

Then Sylvia stood up and walked the few steps it took to get to Lisette on the other side of the living room. She placed her hand on Lisette's shoulder. "Are you okay, Lisette?"

"Yeah, I feel like Roger came back to talk to us today." Lisette's voice was surprisingly calm. "Thank you, Dad, for sharing that."

"No problem, I needed it too," Louis replied. "I've been reading it over and over for the last couple of weeks. I think I've memorized it." He handed the paper to Lisette. "Now, I want you to keep it."

Taking hold of the precious piece of paper, Lisette said, "Thank you, Louis, I'll cherish it."

"We all needed to hear Roger's words today," Sylvia remarked.

CHAPTER 28

That afternoon, Sylvia packed up her suitcases to go back home to her husband. There was a beaming smile on her face. She looked as if a giant weight had been lifted from her. And indeed, a giant weight had been lifted off all of them. Before she left with Louis, she hugged Rebecca for a long time. Then she turned to Lisette and hugged her. Lisette supposed she'd have to get used to the new, cuddlier Sylvia.

"Lisette, thank you for putting up with me. And if you'll have me, I'd like to come here every other Saturday and babysit for Rebecca. That way you could get away for a break and I can see my adorable granddaughter." Sylvia paused but then quickly added, "Visit her, not live with her. You are her mama. And you're a good one too." Sylvia winked.

The corners of Lisette's face lifted into a smile. "Of course, Sylvia, you're welcome any time. You were a lot of help these past few months. I was very nervous about being a mother. I was even considering placing Rebecca over to be adopted." Lisette felt her face grow red with that admission.

Sylvia gasped as her voice raised quite a bit. "No!"

Louis's face looked shocked.

"Well yes, I was considering it, but I'm not anymore." Lisette continued to smile warmly. "You showed me the ropes nicely. Thank you."

Measurable relief showed on Sylvia's and Louis's faces. Sylvia then smiled warmly back at Lisette and said, "You're welcome and I'm just a phone call away. Call any time."

"I will." Lisette reached out to give Sylvia another warm, tight hug.

Louis put his arms around them both and said, "That's my girls."

Louis played the part of reconciler today adeptly, Lisette thought as she watched Sylvia and Louis step out of her front door and head to the elevator.

After Louis and Sylvia's departure, Lisette cleaned and organized the apartment. Soon she would be back at work and it would be nice to have things in tiptop shape before then.

Lisette began straightening up her bedroom and spied the stack of cardboard boxes that had been sitting empty for months in the corner.

She brought the three cardboard boxes into the center of her living room and set them up, open, on the couch. It was time.

Lisette gathered up her high school photo album, her college photo album, and a few framed pictures of Roger and her. She even retrieved the silver-framed wedding picture from her bedroom nightstand.

She smiled, touched her right index finger to her lips and kissed it. Then she moved her finger toward the picture and touched Roger's face before she set the picture down in its new home. She went to get a towel from the linen closet and wrapped up the picture frames. She might want to look at them from time to time, just not every day, that's much too hard.

She noticed various things around the apartment that Roger and she had bought together but she wouldn't pack those things up. They were investing in their future and the future was still here.

She opened her bedroom closet and looked at Roger's side. His gray suit, a few white Oxford shirts, a few polo shirts, a couple pairs of khakis, a couple pairs of black pants, five pairs of jeans, and a few tee shirts.

There was no reason to keep these things. She headed into the kitchen and pulled out a black drawstring plastic bag. She took it back to the bedroom and pulled out all those clothes. Lisette pressed them into the bag which she'd donate to some clothing charity. All except one crisp, white button-up shirt. She laid it out on the bed and unbuttoned the top three buttons. Then she folded the shirt up so that the opening of the neck was on top. She placed the shirt into one of the cardboard boxes. There wasn't anything wrong with keeping one as a treasured memory.

Lisette ran into the bathroom and opened the

medicine cabinet. Still inside was a small Brut deodorant and cologne bottle. She picked them up and brought them into the bedroom. Then she sprayed the white shirt with a couple squirts of Brut. Lisette then lifted the shirt to her face and breathed the scent of Roger. His face drifted into her mind and he was smiling as if he approved.

A couple months ago, she wouldn't have been able to do that without crying. She placed the shirt back into the box and stuffed the deodorant and cologne bottle into the side of the box. Then she firmly pressed the lid on top.

All three boxes went onto the top shelf of her closet. She would not throw any of that stuff away. She was just packing them away for safe keeping. Memories were good, even bittersweet ones. These were the memories of Lisette's first chapter of life but there would be more chapters. Rebecca's next eighteen years would be Lisette's next chapter.

Lisette walked over toward Rebecca's crib under the window and touched Rebecca's little, button nose with her finger.

"And you, my little one, are worth venturing onward."

Over the next week, Lisette enjoyed watching Rebecca before she had to go back to work. It turned out to be sunny most days, so she took Rebecca to the park a lot. She had always been a happy baby but now she seemed even happier or maybe it was Lisette's outlook that was more joyful. Maybe Lisette was smiling more at her baby. Lisette began reading *Rebecca of Sunnybrook Farm* to her. She knew Rebecca couldn't understand yet, but she seemed to enjoy hearing Lisette's voice.

By the end of the week, Lisette was about as ready as she would ever be to go back to work. She made plans for Mrs. Neumeyer, who lived on the floor below her, to watch Rebecca during the daytime. She was a licensed day care provider in her fifties. She only watched three children at a time, so Lisette was grateful that she had an opening for Rebecca.

Periodically, Lisette read the words that Roger had written. She even kept the folded piece of paper in her purse. It felt like a kind of time-honored memorabilia from a far-off time in the past, even though it wasn't so long ago.

The wounds of the past year had finally become healed scars, still noticeable but not as painful.

Lisette knew there was one thing she must do now that she had begun walking a renewed path. She must call Sandra and apologize.

She hit the button for Sandra's name on her cell phone. Lisette was hoping she wouldn't answer, and she could leave a voice mail message.

After three rings, she heard Sandra's ever-friendly voice, "Hello."

Lisette was tempted to hang up out of fear, but she knew Sandra already knew it was her.

"Hello. Lisette?"

Lisette cleared her throat and began. "Sandra... umm... hi."

"Hi," Sandra mimicked.

Lisette paused again. The right words just weren't coming.

"Lisette?" Sandra questioned again.

Still no words.

"Lisette? Are you okay?"

Lisette began. "Sandra, I don't know what to say but... I'm sorry."

"Oh Lisette, I'm sorry too. I never meant to push you into anything."

"You didn't, Sandra, but even if you did, you meant only good things for me." Lisette continued. "I'm sorry for trying to blame you for my anxieties. And I'm sorry for treating you horribly. You didn't deserve any of my insults. I'm so sorry, Sandra."

Sandra's enthusiasm spilled out. "I'm glad you called, Lisette. I should have called you sooner. I wanted to. But... I guess I wanted to give you your space. But Lisette, I missed you."

"I missed you too, Sandra." Relief flooded Lisette's body. She had her friend back.

"Now I really can't wait for you to come back to work. I was worried you might get another job to get away from me. When is your first day back again? Or did you get another job?"

"No, I'll be back, Sandra." Lisette smiled. "Monday,

to be exact."

CHAPTER 29

L isette dropped off Rebecca at Mrs. Neumeyer's apartment for the first time. A few tears formed in Lisette's eyes, but she knew Rebecca was in good hands. Mrs. Neumeyer had been watching children for at least thirty years.

On her way to work, Lisette stopped at Cuppa Joe's for a hot caramel macchiato with extra whipped cream, just because. She wrapped her hands around the beverage to warm them on this forty-some degree day.

At the diner, she noticed a large chocolate cake sitting on the counter. She read the yellow icing, *Welcome back, Lisette*, as Sandra popped out of the kitchen. Bob followed Sandra and they both yelled, "Welcome back!"

Lisette's face grew warm. "You didn't have to do this."

Sandra had baked and iced the cake herself. It was a dark chocolate amaretto cake. Lisette didn't know how they did it but all of them managed to wait for lunchtime to cut that mass of delectable chocolate goodness even though the aroma was overwhelming.

All the customers during the first hour of the lunch rush got a free piece for their dessert. Everyone agreed that it was delicious. Bob even got the idea to start a daily dessert display and let Sandra cook whatever she wanted to display in it. Sandra didn't hesitate at taking him up on his offer.

"That's so great that Bob will let you bake desserts to sell, Sandra. That's a dream come true for you."

Sandra's dark cheeks turned crimson in an atypical display of embarrassment.

"What's that look on your face?" Lisette glanced sideways at her friend.

Sandra's grin grew wider with a tight-lipped, almost smug smile that made Lisette even more curious.

Lisette repeated, "Sandra? What is that strange look on your face?"

"Bob's been listening to more and more of my ideas for the diner. He thinks they are good ideas. It feels good to be appreciated."

Sandra's face still looked like there was more to this story. Lisette's eyes widened as she waited for more information.

"He thinks I bake well, that's all."

Lisette tapped her foot because she knew there was more that Sandra wasn't telling.

Then Sandra burst out, "Bob and I have started dating."

"What?" Lisette grabbed Sandra's left hand with

both of her hands. "Well, well, well, I was right."

Sandra nodded and continued to smile dreamily. "Yeah, you were right. He told me he's been sweet on me for a while now."

"Yeah?" Lisette squealed. "And...I think you've been a little sweet on him too...even if you never said anything."

"Yeah," Sandra concurred as the same wide smile lingered on her face.

"I'm so happy for you, Sandra, no one deserves this happiness more."

"I don't know about that. I think you deserve to be this happy too, Lisette. You've been through so much. Things are turning around for you. I can feel it. You even look livelier than you did before your maternity leave." Sandra continued before Lisette could object. "You deserve something wonderful too."

"Sandra, I had years of immense happiness with Roger. That was wonderful." Lisette spoke matter-of-factly. "Maybe that happiness was so great it was enough for a whole lifetime. Maybe I can live off those wonderful memories."

"There's still more of your life to live, Lisette. And...there's more memories to be made," Sandra urged. "Remember that."

Lisette thought for a moment then answered Sandra with, "That's true. I've also got great happiness to look forward to with Rebecca."

"And?" Sandra's eyes grew wider with anticipation.

"And what?" Happiness with her daughter, Rebecca, was enough for Lisette.

Sandra looked infuriated. "What about David? Until today, he's been to the diner almost every day in the past couple of months and he always asks if I've heard from you and if you're okay."

"David is just a very nice man, that's all." Lisette spoke aloud but then the thought hit her, *a nice man she drove away*. So, any possibility of what Sandra was hinting about was over.

Sandra let out a simple, "Uh huh."

"Sandra, really. You're incorrigible."

"Maybe so but if you can be right about Bob and me, then maybe I can be right about David and you."

Bob walked by them and interrupted, "Okay, you two, get back to work." Bob's smile said he wasn't mad.

"Yes, sir." Sandra gave a mock salute.

Bob just shook his head and widened his eyes at Sandra.

Sandra smirked back at him and then they both cooed at one another.

Lisette smiled at their newfound happiness and wondered if Sandra could be right about David and her. Then reality resettled into her brain and she doubted that could ever happen. There had been too much turbulent water under that bridge. She had been mean to him and he probably wasn't coming back.

Lisette shook her head again. She would never be able to convince Sandra any differently though. Sandra would have to see things her way. Now that she was back, David wouldn't come back into the diner.

Besides, didn't Sandra say he had come into the diner a lot during her absence? Why hadn't he come in that day? Had he looked through the window, saw her, and went elsewhere?

Even though he worked across the street from the diner, she knew she would never see him again.

Her only regret was that they could have at least parted friends.

CHAPTER 30

Every night after work, Lisette got comfortable in the routine of feeding, bathing, and playing with Rebecca. She enjoyed spending as much time with her as possible. She loved her beautiful daughter with a love she couldn't have imagined. At times, she still wondered if she could give Rebecca a proper home all by herself, but she couldn't imagine ever giving her to someone else. She was glad she hadn't gone through with that plan.

Once Rebecca was sound asleep for the night, Lisette also gained another ritual. She read Roger's almost-prophetic writing. It brought her encouragement and hope to go on. Lisette read it once each night. Every time she did, she felt like Roger was sitting right beside her. She liked to picture his warm hand caressing her shoulder as she read as if he was saying, "Honey, you'll be all right."

Thinking of Roger spurring her onward in her life was a nice way for her to fall asleep. Roger would want her to be happy, just like Sandra always said.

That night, however, Lisette noticed something new in the reading.

There is a season for everything, Lord, and I have tried to make the most of my seasons. I try to encourage my parents. I try to encourage my girlfriend. I even try to encourage acquaintances I may never see again. I haven't done it perfectly, Lord, and only time will tell if you are happy with how I spent my life but until then I'll continue encouraging people.

If I don't have much longer on this earth, Lord, help me live for others and help meet their needs before my own. Help me remember that you are a God of love, first and foremost, and I should be an imitator of that love to people. Thank you, Lord, for showing me the way.

Roger was an encouraging person. Lisette had always known that. He had encouraged her in high school, college, and in their brief marriage. He had always given her hope and strength to carry on.

She had also seen him encourage countless other people during the time she knew him. Sally, the young girl with a slight case of downs syndrome, in their high school. Tim, the shortest kid in their grade. Maria, the smart but timid valedictorian of their graduating class. It seemed like every person that Roger met was better off after speaking with him. And the list didn't stop there.

Lisette could go on for a long time citing the many people that Roger had encouraged. During their college years, he tutored many, not for extra money but just to help. Yes, Roger was kind and helpful every chance he got.

One time they had just finished lunch at McDonald's and on their way out, Roger noticed a young, disheveled man who was not much older than they were. He was leaning against the wall, holding a tattered McDonald's paper cup with a few coins in it. The young man was holding up the cup, but he wasn't asking any passerby for money. It seemed like he had given up.

Roger grabbed Lisette's hand and led her back into the restaurant where he bought a double cheeseburger, fries, and a soda. Then they walked back outside where Roger handed the meal to the young man with a nod and a smile.

The young man took the items, smiled, and said, "Thank you. I'm hungry."

Roger and Lisette both smiled. But Roger didn't stop there. He asked the young man If he wanted company while he ate his meal. The young man spoke a timid yes so, all three of them walked back into the McDonald's to sit and talk. Roger and Lisette found out that his name was Bill and his parents had kicked him out years before when they couldn't get him to stop using drugs. Bill had assured them he had stopped doing drugs at some point since leaving their house, but he thought it was too late for him. He had messed up his life.

Roger told him, "God has made second chances a common thing in this world. You can always change and go on a different path." Roger also tried to convince him he should go back to his parents' house. Bill said he would think about it and Roger prayed for him right then and there.

Someone else that Lisette knew was a kind, encouraging, and a helpful person. David! She wondered if maybe, just maybe, Roger had arranged something with God to bring another encourager into her life to help her. It brought a smile to her face to think of that possibility. That God would care about her so much that he would bring another person like Roger into her life when she needed it. Lisette sent up a silent but grateful thank you prayer. God didn't feel distant anymore.

She also wondered if maybe it was time. But had she grieved enough? Does a specific amount of time mean that she'd grieved sufficiently? In a way, there would always be a soft spot where the pain would always remain. But maybe, just maybe, God was saying she could go on with life even though she'd never, ever forget. Lisette smiled at the idea of living again. She felt like she had permission now.

But what good was this revelation if she'd already blown it with her new encourager? It had been almost a week since she'd been back to work and David hadn't come into the diner once. The only possibility in Lisette's mind was that he didn't want to see her anymore. She had wanted him to go away, and he did. She got her wish.

Lisette sighed and began another prayer.

Lord, in my limited knowledge of you and the bible, I seem to remember stories of you giving second chances to people. I know that Roger believed in them and he knew the bible more than me. Can I have one of those second chances? I've learned a lot of lessons and I think I would handle it better this time. Amen.

◆ ◆ ◆

Lisette talked with Sandra off and on throughout the breakfast shift about her revelation. When she first brought it up, a huge grin plastered itself on Sandra's face and didn't seem to want to leave.

"Girl, it's about time!"

"Sandra, don't look at me like that. How do you know for sure that this could work or that he's even still interested?" Lisette looked at her friend skeptically.

"Well, I think an outsider can see these things better than the person who is involved. You saw me and Bob as a couple before I did." Sandra tilted her head in the direction of the kitchen.

"That was different. I saw Bob flirting with you day in and day out." Lisette chuckled. "And...I even saw you flirting back. It was easy to figure that out."

Sandra gave a knowing look. "Hello...I saw that same thing in David and you. It was glaringly obvious to everyone but you."

Lisette pressed her lips together and considered what her friend had seen all along. She sighed. "Maybe. But it's too late." Lisette looked around the room and gestured. "I've been back to work and he isn't coming back in. I ruined everything."

"Not necessarily, girl. He could still come back in. Maybe he's just giving you some space to get back into your work routine. Maybe he's just busy at work, too busy to take a lunch. Or the top reason could be that he thinks he'll be bothering you if he comes back in because of all that has come to pass." Sandra shrugged. "Lisette, I don't really know why but I think he'll come back in sometime. And I'll pray that it is soon. God is bigger than misunderstandings and he often gives second chances."

Lisette shook her doubting head, but she hoped that Sandra was right. She used the term second chances just like Lisette had prayed last night. "I hope you're right. I really do."

The lunch rush came and went with no sign of David. Every time the bell on the front door tinkled, Lisette looked up. At two o'clock, there were only a few customers left and she started her clean-up duties by wiping down the counters and tables thoroughly. Sandra came by a few times and placed a gentle hand on the small of Lisette's back.

CHAPTER 31

Lisette wiped down a table as she squinted at the brightness of the afternoon sun. She saw a man leaving the building across the street and squinted harder. The man headed in the diner's direction and Lisette thought it could be David. Was he coming to the diner?

Bob's voice called the hamburger platter that her last customer had ordered, and she moved to the back of the diner to get it. As she carried the plate over to the gray-haired man in jeans and a dark blue polo shirt, she heard a horrible screech outside.

Sandra ran toward the front of the diner and then blurted out, "I think a person was just hit by a car."

It was all that Lisette could do to keep the plate of steaming hot food steady, but somehow, she managed to set it down in front of her customer.

Then she walked a few steps toward the front of the restaurant, but something stopped her from going any further. Could David have been hit by that car?

A warmth rose in Lisette's throat along with nausea. She pulled out a turquoise padded chair and sat down to avoid passing out. She didn't know if she could handle another person getting into a car accident.

Sandra moved toward Lisette. "Are you okay? You look pale."

Lisette could barely speak. "David...was...out there. I...I...saw him."

Sandra's eyes grew big. "I couldn't see who it was, Lisette."

"But...I thought I saw him. He seemed to be heading in this direction."

Sandra spoke up. "We cannot assume that, Lisette. We can't."

"But..."

"No, we can't assume that. Are you sure you even saw him?"

Lisette nodded. "Well...I'm pretty sure."

Sandra shook her head. "Well, we still can't assume the worst. We don't know."

Shallow breaths came from Lisette's throat. Just like with Roger, she could be at fault for another tragedy.

An ambulance showed up and parked between the accident and the diner so now they couldn't see any details. Sandra whispered prayers out loud for the person's healing, whoever it was. Lisette was still shaking. She couldn't pray or even think. But she sent up the one-word prayer of *Help* many times in her head.

After what seemed like hours but was actually only twenty to thirty minutes, the ambulance pulled away with its lights on heading to the hospital. The chaos on the street in front of the diner calmed down to normal.

Lisette headed for the ladies' room to splash water on her face. The cool water revived her some. Lisette didn't know David was hit by that car. She also didn't know he wasn't. There would always be unknowns in life. Something could happen to David just like something terrible happened to Roger. Nothing was guaranteed.

She had to trust that God could get her through anything that happened in her life. He was there for her during the intense grief over Roger even when she didn't feel it. He was there and brought people into her life to help her. That didn't mean she wouldn't ever grieve again over anything else. But it did mean she could live again after any grief that came along. There was a time to grieve. There was a time to live. And God would help no matter which stage she was in.

Lisette left the ladies' room much refreshed even though she still didn't know what had happened that afternoon.

Lisette reached down to pick up a napkin that had fallen on the floor. When she stood back up, the bell over the door tinkled.

It was David and he walked over to her. Relief flooded her face. He wasn't in that accident.

"I'm a little late. Is lunch still being served?" David asked with his usual smile like it was a normal day.

"Oh, David, there was an accident out front and I thought it might have been you."

David placed a comforting hand on Lisette's shoulder. "No, it wasn't me, Lisette, but that is why I'm extra late today. I was heading here, and I saw a homeless man jaywalk into the road. I could tell there wasn't enough time for him to cross, so I yelled out, 'Sir' to get his attention. I thought maybe he'd turn around quickly and come back to the sidewalk." David gulped. "But...he didn't come back. He went forward and then the corner of a brown SUV slammed into him and knocked him to the ground."

Lisette placed her hand over her mouth. "Oh no. Was the man still alive? I'm sorry you had to witness that."

David nodded. "They took him to the hospital in the ambulance, but the medics thought he should be okay."

A long sigh escaped Lisette's mouth. "Oh good."

David smiled as he took a seat at his usual table. Then he added, "By the way, welcome back to work, Lisette."

He was acting like nothing bad had happened between them. Could he have forgiven her so easily? If he had forgiven Lisette, then why did he wait so long to come back into the diner?

Lisette swallowed back her confusion. None of that mattered now. The only thing that mattered was that he was back and maybe she'd get that second chance. She smiled back at him. "You're not late. We serve food all afternoon." She turned from him to get him a menu.

Sandra came by and said, "Hi David, welcome back."

Lisette saw a wink from Sandra to David and wondered what it meant.

"Thanks, Sandra." David remarked and then he perused the menu.

Lisette wiped down a nearby table. It was taking him more time than usual to decide. When Lisette finished wiping down another table, she looked around the room to make sure that the other customer had left. Then she stepped closer to David's table. Even Sandra had gone into the kitchen. Lisette felt as if God had arranged for the two of them to be alone. She sat down next to David. He gave her an odd look. Lisette didn't blame him. She hadn't been very consistent with him.

Lisette breathed in a large dose of courage and began. "David, I'm so sorry for treating you so badly. You were nothing but nice and I practically slapped you in the face multiple times."

"Lisette, you don't have to..." David tried to interrupt her.

Lisette reached out and put a finger against his lips. "Shh...of course I do. I was horrible, and you deserved better. I'm very sorry for treating you so badly."

David smiled and looked relieved. "Thank you."

Lisette saw the relief in David's face and took another cleansing breath, so she could continue. "David, I also need to say something else."

"What? Is something wrong? Is Rebecca okay? Are you okay?"

"No, nothing is wrong, Rebecca is great. David. In fact, there's a lot right. Very, very right."

David squinted his eyes in a silent question.

"I have this feeling I'd like to get to know you better." Lisette looked shyly away from her demonstrative statement. "And...I want to...and...I'm even okay with it. I think it's okay. It's really okay." Relief flooded her body as she continued to give herself permission to live again. It felt good. It felt like she was coming out of a dark tunnel and a bright light was beckoning her.

David reached for Lisette's left hand and cupped it with both of his hands. "Lisette, I was attracted to you from day one and the more I got to know you the more I really liked you. I knew there would be hurdles and I knew it wouldn't be easy. But...I also knew something was holding you back. You know I'm familiar with that kind of grief. I should have kept myself from pushing you though." David looked down but then continued. "I prayed that you would gain peace for yourself. But secondly, I also prayed, a little selfishly, that you'd like me too."

"I do...I really do. And I have that peace you prayed about. Most of all, I don't feel bitter against God anymore. I know that He loves me even though Roger was taken from me. God never left me even though I left him." Spilling out her revelations made them seem even more real.

"I'm glad to hear that, Lisette." David leaned forward and kissed her lips. Lisette felt the same electricity of their previous kiss and her lips pressed back.

When their lips parted, Lisette spoke, "Do you mind if we take everything slow? One step at a time into a different season. I think I can handle that."

"No, I don't mind that, Lisette. I'm just glad I get a second chance." David lifted and squeezed Lisette's hand.

There was that phrase again. "I'm glad for second chances too, David."

Two weeks later, Lisette and David walked out of her apartment building on an unseasonably warm December day. David was taking Lisette and Rebecca to the park. Lisette placed Rebecca into her car seat.

Lisette remembered the young couple that had come into the diner many months ago. The ones that were cooing and loving their new baby. Maybe Lisette would have a chance at that kind of life after all. The kind of life that seemed so out of reach for so long.

Everything seemed to be falling into place in this new season. A different season. A season that doesn't negate the first one.

The End

<<<<>>>>

ABOUT THE AUTHOR

Jennifer Heeren loves to write stories and articles that bring hope and encouragement to others. She wants to live in such a way that people are encouraged by her writing and her attitude. Her cup is always at least half-full, even when circumstances aren't ideal. She regularly contributes to Crosswalk.com. She lives near Atlanta, Georgia with her husband. Visit her at www.jenniferheeren.com.

Made in the USA
Monee, IL
25 January 2022